CHAMELEON

Revised

BY:

JACKIE McCONNELL

ESCAPE HATCH PRODUCTION LLC.

Published in the United States of America by:

ESCAPE HATCH PRODUCTION LLC.

ESCAPE HATCH PRODUCTION LLC.

TWISTED
PAPER TRAIL
FAMILY MATTERS
UNFORESEEN OCCURRENCE
JOURNEY TO THE BEGINNING
THE PINEAL TREASURES
MY JOURNEY THUS FAR(Autobiography)
PLANT THE SEED
THE PAINTING
PLOTTERS
DEADLY TRADE-OFF
TERMINAL PAYOFF
BLACK RAVINE
HONEY(CAT)
TWO-FACED
BLACK MAGIC WOMAN(VOODOO CHILD SERIES)
THE LAWYER
RESURRECTION
TATTOO
CROSSROADS
TEEN DRONES
IMMACULATE DECEPTION
SEE NO EVIL
TAKE OUT THE GARBAGE
ROGUE NATION/SPLIT DECISION
THE GIFT
THE CORE VALUE
WHAT ARE THE CHANCES?
TRANSPARENT OASIS

NOTICE

This is a work of fiction. Names, character, places, and incidents either are the product of the author's imagination, or are used fictitiously. Any resemblance to actual persons, living or dead, events, or locales is entirely coincidental.

People change persona, shapes, and colors. The direct bond is inhabited by Chameleons. It is said the connection with our reptilian skin texture is a direct link to these traits.

THE BOOK OF COUNTLESS THOUGHTS

1.

Shottenville, Louisiana at the predawn hours on a Saturday is an enchanting time for the young couple that frequents this area. The location was Old Man Cutter's Cornfield. During the summer solstice of early August, the temperature was humidly warm. There was a warm southwest breeze coming in from the Gulf. It illuminated the scent of the sun-ripened stalks of corn. The sweet scent was pleasant. The aroma accentuated the mood.

Sonny looked up at the clear nocturnal sky. Its deep purple hue, along with a full moon in the backdrop, was enchanting. Sonny was the most popular boy in Ridge Mount High School. His body was naturally well developed and proportioned. He held natural athleticism and played varsity football. As a wide receiver, his future was promising. Sonny's cornrow braided hairstyle silhouetted against the backdrop of corn stalks that were seemingly omnipresent. His dark skin revealed perspiration as moonlight cascaded from his huge presence. Amber was sprawled beneath him on a colorful, quilted blanket. The cover was kept in his brand new pickup truck. The vehicle was an undocumented gift forwarded to Sonny as an incentive to make the right choice to play for a particular college upon graduation. Scouts from around the country were trying to persuade him to sign with their schools.

Amber was his unofficial girlfriend due to the distorted social climate in that part of the country. The racial divide caused the region to be at an unrest. Amber was of a different ethnicity. Her parent's held liberal viewpoints. It resulted in her open-mindedness on the subject. As a result, she believed love conquered all. It was one of the reasons they kept their tryst obscured from prying eyes. The plan was to complete their education. Afterward, they would reveal their love to the world. Their philosophy was love all people. Amber Wainwright was a beautiful girl with a curvy figure. She was bestowed with greenish-blue eyes set in almond shaped sockets. Her creamy skin was smooth and soft. Sonny and Amber's complexions contrasted immensely as they held one another in an intimate embrace. Amber's natural blonde hair was done in a stylish French braid.

Sonny was in a fervent mood. Being close to Amber excited him tremendously. He loved her dearly. His wanting passion for her was strong; at times it was uncontrollable. Sonny fought hard with the emotion. Nonetheless, he wouldn't let his clouded feelings dictate their future of happiness together. Neither experienced physical sexual relations. Sonny held Amber in high regard. It was for that reason he hadn't made love to her as of yet. Although she insisted on a regular bases, he wouldn't give in. Everything had to be perfect as she was to him. Sonny had a five-year plan that would give them the life they deserved.

Amber's voice was seductive. "Sonny, I am ready." She looked up at him with the full moon overhead making her want him even more. "Take me, I don't care what anyone says about us being together."

Sonny kissed her full, puffy, round lips. "I know what you mean. Believe me, I feel the same way you do. You have no idea of the type of control used to battle my desires for you. I want you in the worst way. When it does happen, I want it to be right. We both have promising careers ahead of us. If given the proper cultivation we can go far."

"We have protection."

"There is no guarantee we will be protected. Once the process of parenthood has begun I will not allow an abortion, nor will there be any regrets. Believe me Amber, you'll thank me later." His gaze was that of sincerity.

Amber could feel his stare as it bore directly into her being. She felt as if she was transported to another time and place when she was in the presence of Sonny. They spoke freely with one another. There was nothing that needed to be guessed when it came to their needs and desires. "Okay, can you please dowse this burning sensation between my legs? Please?" Her voice was childlike and seductive. Amber loved the way he satisfied her orally. Sonny held nothing back when he was with her; he only wanted to please her in anyway possible.

Suddenly, the sound of corn stalks rattled in the far distance. Sonny and Amber remained motionless as they listened attentively.

"W-what do you think that was?" Amber's voice was queazy.

"Maybe it's just an owl preying on a field rat."

The sound resumed. This time, an unusual faint sound emitted amongst the dense stalks of corn.

"It sounded like an animal."

"It could be just someone trying to scare us."

"Well, it's working," retorted Amber truthfully.

"Don't worry babe. There's nothing to worry about. I will always protect you." Sonny stood. His huge frame silhouetted against the moon in the backdrop. He placed his shirt on. "Stay here. I'm gonna check it out. I'm sure it's nothing to be concerned about."

"No! Don't leave me here alone!" Amber stood. Her dress was hiked around her thighs. She began to straighten her clothing. "I'm going with you."

With Sonny in the lead, they headed into the maze of corn. The warm temperature exaggerated their anxiety. Sonny listened as he moved forward. All was quiet at the moment. A gentle breeze moved the leaves on the stalks. They stopped to listen. Nothing stirred.

Suddenly, an eerie sound emitted. It resonated from behind them. Amber was totally frightened. Internally, her glands secreted endorphins at a normal level. Suddenly, high levels of adrenaline was exchanged from extreme fear of the unknown. She was unaware that her scent permeated the air. Only sensitive nasals were able to detect such a scent. Some species perceived the aroma as delightful.

"Let's get out of here." Amber's voice trembled, so did her body.

"Don't worry, I won't let anything happen to you." Sonny held her near. "Maybe you're right. Let's get out of here. It's probably someone playing a sick prank." Taking Amber's hand, Sonny led her in the direction of the vehicle.

SKEEECH! The loud shriek was unnerving. It was a sound they didn't recognize, a noise they've never heard. Sonny's instinct indicated something unusual was happening. Instinctively, he felt there was imminent danger lurking about. A strange intuition gnawed at him mentally, it gave recognition that the sound was not of this world.

"Com' on, let's move!" he commanded. The full moon was the only illumination allowing them the ability to navigate and seek refuge from the unknown. The sound of their feet pattered on the cultivated dirt. The flopping sound of stalks being pushed aside by the duo was profound.

The vehicle was now one hundred yards away. Abruptly, the sound of pursuit by the unknown assailant was prevalent in the background.

"Run Amber!" shouted Sonny. He remained in the rear of Amber. To his thinking, he would protect her from any mishap.

They were now 50 yards to the clearing where the pickup truck was parked. The two ran purposefully. Sonny felt his legs being snagged. The vise-like grip on his limbs caused him to lose his balance. The fall reminded him of an illegal tackle experienced on the football field. Amber heard the commotion and slowed her stride in order to look back. Because of the nocturnal setting, her vision was impaired.

"Go! Don't stop! Run Amber!" Hearing the urgent commands from Sonny caused her to run forward. Seconds afterward, an eerie cry of anguish resounded in the quiet night. A harsh shriek followed. It sent a shockwave through Amber's body.

Twenty-five feet to the clearing, Amber pushed onward. Hysteria set in. Her world became surreal. Instinctively, she knew something terrible happened to Sonny. His voice was no longer audible. The paranormal encounter was something she couldn't describe with words. Amber felt whatever was out there was not earthly.

Five feet from the clearing, Amber was able to make out the outline of the pickup truck. The sight of it gave her hope. She knew Sonny always kept the keys in the sun visor above the passenger side seat.

One foot to the clearing, Amber spread the leafy corn stalks aside in an attempt to exit the large patch. The unthinkable happened. Amber felt her feet being snatched from under her. Losing her balance, she fell hard to the dirt ground. The action happened quick and forcefully. Amber wasn't prepared to protect herself from the fall. She came down hard face first losing consciousness. Her last vision was the ground rushing to meet her face before blankness permeated her being. Amber's unconscious body was dragged deeper into the cornfield. Another loud shriek resounded in the warm darkness. Unknown to Amber, her virginity had been stolen by the unidentifiable entity. In the process, the creature's sharp, razor-like fingernail marked her fragile skin. The creature left a tell-tale scar on her body to signify she'd been forcefully abused.

2.

Officer Wainwright received a call from his wife notifying him that Amber hadn't return home. Her ten o'clock curfew had long expired. The act was unlike her character. Officer Wainwright was a proud father and police officer. He served the community of Shottenville, Louisiana for a decade. The hysterical nature of the call disturbed him gravely because of the affectionate pursuit Amber and Sonny held for one another.

The Wainwrights raised their daughter to see character in a person, not the color of their skin. Since moving to the deep south from the inner-city of East Philadelphia, they were forced to witness the biases that were deep-rooted in the territory. It didn't bother them that Amber displayed affection toward an African American boy. After talking with him, they knew Sonny was a respectable person who was serious about his athletic career. When Officer

Wainwright first met Sonny, he was truly impressed by the young man's character and mannerism. Sonny displayed a sense of direction for his future. Their man-to-man talks were very sincere. Conclusively, both men held Amber's welfare in high regards.

Officer Wainwright searched for Amber. His first thought was to visit Sonny's home on Scepter Lane. The townhouse was located in a subdivision on a cul-de-sac. The block held identically structured homes. The only differences between the dwellings were the diverse house numbers. As Officer Wainwright stopped his vehicle in front of Sonny's home, he noticed the new pickup truck wasn't in the driveway. He decided to check into the matter further. Exiting the vehicle, Officer Wainwright adjusted his uniform. He always prided himself on having a neat appearance. For a man in his late 50's, Officer Wainwright was in good physical condition. He maintained himself on a well-balanced diet, exercise and rest. He looked years younger than he actually was.

Amber was a perfectly blended mixture of both her parents. Her well toned body and spirited drive, was attributed from his genetic traits. Her beauty, skin tone, and full natural blonde hair were her mother's gifts.

Officer Wainwright knocked on the door. Thereafter, a light illuminated through the closed drapes at the window. The sound of the peephole cover resonated from the other side of the door. The lock latch sounded on the quiet block. The high-pitch squeal of the screen door shrieked as it opened, its need for oil was apparent. Standing in front of him was a dark complexioned woman. She wore a dark green, cotton robe. Her hair was covered by a silky, green cloth. She was very attractive. Her curvy body silhouetted through the robe. She wore no makeup on her beautiful face. Her skin was flawless. The woman's eyes were hazelnut brown. They were set in monolid shaped eye sockets. The epicanthic folds revealed her mixed heritage. Recognizing the caller produced a smiled that exposed perfect, white teeth.

Suddenly, a disconcerting thought occurred causing the woman's expression to change. She stood in front of the door with one hand on her hip, the other closing the upper part of her robe. "Is there something wrong? Where is Sonny?" She suddenly felt a deep chill within. The sensation reached her core.

"That's why I'm here. When Amber didn't make her curfew, the wife got worried. So here I am." Officer Wainwright gazed toward his feet. He was obviously embarrassed. He knew he was intruding at a late hour.

"I haven't seen either of them. Sonny has a test in the morning and knows I don't accept that kind of behavior."

"Maybe it's nothing to worry about. You know how teenagers can be."

"Hmm." That was her sound reaction. "I sure do. I know that I'm goin' to break my foot off in his ass when I see him." Her voice displayed displeasure and irritability.

"I am sure they're somewhere close by. They probably forgot all about the time. I am going to look for them. I am sure his red truck shouldn't be too hard to locate. I'll bring him back personally." A thought occurred to him. It caused him to chuckle.

"What's so funny?"

"I-I was just thinking about breaking my foot off in Amber's ass also." The two burst into laughter.

***

Officer Wainwright scoured the neighborhood looking for Sonny and Amber. He visited all the haunts the youngsters attended. It was now 2:30 am. All the social places were now closed. The red pickup truck was nowhere to be spotted. His wife had called again for the countless time. Officer Wainwright placed a call to dispatch. He requested an all-points-bulletin for Sonny. He explained his daughter and Sonny were missing.

Another hour passed slowly. No clue existed. Officer Wainwright began to fear the inevitable. He tried to prepare himself for such an instance, only there was no way to begin. All of a sudden, a high-pitched squelch sounded from the dispatcher on the two-way radio. The abruptness of the noise caused him to jolt in his seat. The discordant sound was intensified in the confined space of the squad car.

"QT-four. The vehicle request has been located at Old Man Cutter's corn patch. Over?"

Officer Wainwright didn't hesitate to respond. "QT-four. Copy. En route. E-T-A 15 minutes. Over and out." The transmission was terminated.

Three squad cars with their emergency lights flashing illuminated the area around the red pickup truck. All three officers were smoking cigarettes. A bluish-gray cloud lingered overhead resembling a halo. Officer Wainwright exited the vehicle to join the circle of officers. The contrast of the vehicles illuminated against the backdrop of darkness was profound.

"What do we have Hal?"

Hal was a short, heavyset officer. His oval-shape and pudgy features were distinctive. He spoke with a southern twang. "This 'ere is that colored boyz truck. No sign of Amber. I told you them nig-" He hesitated from finishing his sentence because he was aware Officer Wainwright didn't have the same viewpoint as the others. He didn't share their biased ideology of the blacks. "Them people are nothin' but trouble. You should 'ave put a halt to him seein' yo' daughter."

"Hal, the key word is mine. Amber isn't your daughter. She's mine." Officer Wainwright walked to the front of the truck and placed a hand on the hood. "This truck has been here for a while, the engine is cold." He looked down at the ground. Using his flashlight, Officer Wainwright began to trace the footprints left in the dirt that led into the cornfield. The other officers looked on feeling self-conscious because they hadn't thought of it first. "Com' on, let's see if we can find them."

With their vehicles in the clearing, and the colorful flashing lights illuminating the entrance, the officers headed into the cornfield. Beams of light danced around the darkness as they used flashlights to search for Amber and Sonny. Hal kept his hand near his holstered weapon. Following the trail of footprints, they searched onward.

"Look!" exclaimed an officers. His finger was pointed. The other officers rushed over to investigate. Their beams of light were trained on the area in question. "Looks like there was a struggle right here." They inspected the disturbed stalks. Some looked as if they were completely pulled out of the ground.

"Damn! It took some strength to do that."

"I told you that nigger wasn't any good," retorted Hal.

Upon further search, a sneaker was found on a mound where a stalk sprang. One of the officers held it up with a leather, gloved hand. He displayed it to the group.

"Yes! That belongs to my daughter." Unholstering his weapon, Officer Wainwright began searching purposefully.

Minutes into the search, they discovered the unthinkable. They came across a motionless body of a female. She was naked and covered in an unknown slimy substance. Her body was bloody and bruised. Further investigation revealed it was Amber Wainwright. The officers went into defensive action. Two of officers pointed their weapons into the unknown darkness. Officer Wainwright searched for a pulse. Somewhat relieved, he felt a faint throbbing sensation in her neck. Her body was covered by Officer Wainwright's uniform shirt. Another officer called for medical assistance on the two-way radio.

"There's no time!" Officer Wainwright lifted his daughter from the dirt ground into his embrace. It took every ounce of restraint to remain focused and professional. Tears and anger ascended from within. He rushed through the intricate maze of corn toward the clearing and dancing lights from the awaiting vehicles.

An intense display of lights and sounds illuminated the ghostly highway as the four-vehicle convoy rushed onward with their sirens blaring at full volume toward the only hospital in town.

3.

Lutheran Medical Center was the only medical facility in the area of Shottenville. They were 100 miles from New Orleans. From the time of Amber's unofficial arrival, she was given precedence as a courtesy to her father.

A full workup was given to Amber. The results were reassuring. A doctor dressed in olive-green colored scrubs entered the waiting area. Officer Wainwright was pacing the floor and devouring cups of hot black coffee. His fellow officers remained with him as long as they could before being called to duty. Drinking his fifth cup of sugarless, black coffee, Officer Wainwright's mind was in a preoccupied state. He tried to put together what occurred. There were too many missing pieces. The words of Officer Hal resonated in his mind. The voice tried to give logic to its bias meaning. He fought hard because he didn't want to believe Sonny took advantage of his little girl. Witnessing the doctor approach changed his thoughts to hopefulness.

Officer Wainwright rushed toward the doctor. "Please doc, is my little girl gonna be alright?" His voice was edgy, his mind was cloudy from the caffeine.

"Officer Wainwright your daughter is a fighter. Physically, there is nothing broken. She has suffered some lacerations. There is something else...." The doctor hesitated in order to choose his words correctly.

"What is it doctor?" Officer Wainwright eyed him suspiciously.

"We found blood at the vaginal opening. Upon further investigation, we discovered that your daughter's hymen has been separated. It looks to be violently afflicted."

"Doc, you've lost me. What are you saying?"

"Your daughter was raped. We're doing a DNA sampling of the discharge found inside of her."

"That f**kin' bastard Sonny!" His scream of was deafening. Officer Wainwright's world began to unravel.

Daylight showered the landscape. When Sonny never returned, an all-points-bulletin was put out for his arrest in the neighboring counties. Officer Wainwright was met at the cornfield by a forensic team. The daylight produced clues that went unnoticed last night. There were blood samples, foreign hair samples, and a slimy substance near the scene. Upon further inspection into the patch, they found what appeared to be bloody clothing. The material was ripped and shredded. The newly discovered evidence was sent to the laboratory for identification purposes.

Officer Wainwright returned to the hospital to visit with Amber. He entered the room to find her conscious. He noticed intravenous tubes protruding from her left arm and right inner wrist. Bruises were evident on her face and arms. Anger arose within.

"How is my princess doing?" He took a seat near the bed. Amber stared straight ahead. It was as if she didn't notice her father was in the room. Her gaze was reflective. Amber's attention was focused ahead as if she could see directly through the colorless wall. "Baby, I need to ask you something. Did Sonny rape you?" He stared at his daughter awaiting a reply. He knew the timing was wrong but he needed to know. Everything was happening fast. *'That is my little girl and I would do anything to protect her at any cost.'* He waited patiently for an answer.

As if what was asked took seconds to penetrate her murky thoughts, Amber's gaze was now directed toward her father. The mention of Sonny's name in a negative suggestion brought back vivid memories of the prior evening. "No! How could you even think like that? He saved my life. If it wasn't for him...." Her voice was strained. Emotions overwhelmed her. Her father reached out and touched her on the shoulder in an effort to console her. "There was something out there. It attacked us. If you don't believe me look at the scratches on my body." Amber threw back the cover that once obscured her body. Her bruised legs and arms were exposed. "Do you really think Sonny would have done this?"

"Amber please! Listen to yourself! It just doesn't make any sense. Do you realize you're no longer a virgin? Semen was found inside of you."

Amber tried to recollect the moments mentally; she tried to recall the exact events. “No! That is not true. Sonny never touched me. All I know is that something grabbed me as I was trying to escape. Sonny fought if off allowing me the time needed to escape. From that point onward I guess I blanked out.”

“Then how do you know it wasn’t him?”

“Because whatever was out there had him also. I heard his scream, then I heard a bone chilling shriek, a sound that wasn’t like anything I’ve ever heard.”

At that moment the doctor entered the room. “I’m sorry to inform you visiting hours have expired.” The doctor adverted his attention to Amber. “It is time for your medicine young lady. I have to get you out of here. This place is for the sick folks.” He chuckled in an effort to lift her spirits.

4.

Officer Wainwright entered the police laboratory. It was a quaint room that held the necessary equipment needed to do forensic studies. Three employees worked in that section. It was an adequate amount for a township of its size.

"Hey Chuck," stated the only female technician on staff. Her name was Molly Fenson. She was tall, slim, and attractive. "I'm glad you stopped by. My report is concluded. The findings are extraordinary."

"What did you find?"

Molly dropped a file folder on the counter next to a powerful double lensed microscope. Officer Wainwright opened it and began rifling through the pages as Molly explained her findings.

"The blood and clothing belong to Sonny. There is no doubt. We crossed matched them with the DNA from his school records. We can assume that he is dead. The baffling part is there were hair fibers found that we've nothing to cross match with. There is no data to identify its source. It doesn't exist in our database. I took the liberty of sending samples to Washington, DC. We also found saliva. It contains the same DNA that matches the semen found inside of your daughter. Still, we can't identify it with any person on file. I even checked with the international databases. Nothing comes up. One thing we know for sure, it's not Sonny's fluid."

'Amber was telling the truth. But what raped her?' Officer Wainwright adverted his attention to Molly. "Thank you Molly, I am going to find more to go on." Officer Wainwright exited the building. He headed toward Old Man Cutter's cornfield. *'Maybe there's something we've overlooked.'*

***

The cornfield seemed less threatening in the daylight hours. The lime-green stalks along with the rows of yellow corn were seemingly endless. Everything that was obscured hours ago in the nocturnal setting was now exposed. Officer Wainwright wandered through the intricate maze of cornrows toward the inner corridors. He headed toward the nucleus. As he neared the center, an indescribable stench hovered in the air. The scent of natural sweet corn was mixed with a foreign stench.

Officer Wainwright noticed a foreign object obscured from sight. It was positioned between a cluster of stalks. He moved closer wincing at the sight. It was the remnant of an unidentifiable body. The cadaver was skinless. The internal organs, although exposed were still in formation. It was a gelatinous substance; a clumped mass of pink, red, and black. The direct exposure to oxygen caused the internal organs to decompose, turning them darker. Malodorous stench magnified immensely as moments passed.

Officer Wainwright placed a handkerchief over his nose to filter the putrid scent. He inched close enough to view the remains. *'What the hell is going on?'* Retrieving his cellphone from his pocket, Officer Wainwright dialed. Connecting with dispatch, he notified them of the recent find. A forensic team was dispatched to the scene.

GENESIS

[1895]

5.

After the French Revolutionary War, the French claimed the majority of the vast land of Louisiana. The social conditions had become unsettling. There were now different cultures and languages in the region. No one understood which government upheld the laws. The results were chaotic. President Jefferson made the purchase of Louisiana from the French at four cents an acre for all 828 thousand square miles. During this time, the slave revolt in Haiti had just begun. Borders were set in place to dissuade other slaves from uprising during the amalgamation of slave owners from other territories. They were there to capitalize on human flesh.

During the Civil War, slaves were forced to fight on both sides of the warring nations. Family members were forced to kill one another depending what side of the armies they'd been purchased into. After the settling of the territories in Louisiana, some of the slaves dispersed running from the appalling abuse of human rights. Some found escape through the swamplands and bayous.

Dwanka, a third generation slave from the Massi tribe, was among them. She was from a proud people of West Africa that was located on the North Atlantic coast. Dwanka, a vibrant, young, African girl filled with ideas acquired from reading books. The slave master's daughter secretly taught Dwanka to read. The reading brought them closer together. It was their secret to cherish forever. Dwanka read books about the freedom in the north. She read about a location called Mason-Dixon line. She learned it separated Maryland, a slave state with Pennsylvania, a free state. After careful planning, Dwanka ran away from her owner. Her only regret was she couldn't tell her best friend goodbye. The years of abuse had begun to be too much for her to withstand. Dwanka was emotionally abused. She was forced to labor in the hot sun until sunset, only to repeat the mistreatment that very next morning.

Dwanka had been separated from her biological family during an auction of slaves at the town square. It was an event that was embedded in her cognizance. The awful scent of blood, urine, feces, and death associated with the slave trade, lingered within her being. Today, the last straw of her patience was tested. She wouldn't withstand another evening of torment. Dwanka secretly hid food rations during the past weeks. The rations included water, food, and other supplies she covertly got her hands on. She wrapped them in a tablecloth and hid the items in the woods. Dwanka decided to navigate at night with the use of the moonlight. She read about ships at sea doing the same. She was also informed about the use of a bright light named the Northern Star. The thought of it caused her to smile.

Using garlic cloves, Dwanka bathed herself in the pungent aroma. She learned from reading the reek would thwart her natural scent from the bloodhounds. She knew the captors would use her clothing to pick up a scent.

Dwanka found herself in the heart of the wetlands. She was now exhausted. Her food supply was depleted. Fear began to infiltrate her thoughts. *'Maybe I should have stayed on the plantation. I don't know what I was thinking, or what to expect.'* Nightfall cascaded upon the marsh emitting an eerie presence. Frightening and unfamiliar sounds of foreign animals and insects resonated in the stillness of the night. Small eyes illuminated from the intense moonlight. Pairs of eyes moved out of the water. Through reading, Dwanka was aware alligators, beavers, and the native garfish infested the water. She had no way to gauge her distance of travel. Doubt crept into her being and caused her to second guess her direction. At times, because of hunger, every thought was questionable.

Dwanka was unable to continue further because the depletion of energy. She stopped at a mound that was slightly above the wet swamp. Although it was soggy on the surface, Dwanka took refuge at that location. Using a tree for a backrest and sat quietly. She remained still absorbing the unfamiliar sights and sounds of her surroundings.

She listened to the foreign sounds. It was her efforts to avoid being surprised by them. Dwanka found herself succumbing to her exhausted mind and body. Using the moonlight, Dwanka studied her fingers. She noticed they were in an advance stage of pruning. The low temperature of the evening made the water more chilling. It lowered her body temperature tremendously. Hypothermia began setting in. Dwanka closed her eyes to embrace the inevitable. Things quieted for Dwanka. She no longer felt the cold. Sleep was all she sought. Her body went into a comatose state.

A few feet from where she sat, a pair of eyes appeared from the murky water. The eyes were starry orbs. The eyelids were oblong giving the eyeballs a saucer shape. The oddity was the two orbs moved independently of each other. They had the ability to view two separate locations simultaneously. The marvel was in the fact the eyelids were one piece with small slits to expose the colorful pupils. The illumination was that of cat eyes. The creature's eyes reflected off of the moonlight. Instead of them blinking and closing from top to bottom, this creature's blinking was done from the inner side sweeping shut across the eye. Two separate shutters on each side of the socket met in the middle. If Dwanka were fully conscious at that moment, she would have been terrified. The creature's body remained hidden in the water as it kept one trained eye on Dwanka and the other on its surroundings. It had been watching the girl for days. It fed off of her emotions and instinctive undercurrent of responses. Such as fear, hope, anger, and the will to survive. The creature was part of a metamorphosis, a prototype in the making. Its sharp survival instincts converged with an enhanced cognitive possession.

The lizard-like creature sensed the life force ebbing out of the body of its prey. In natural conditions, insects would be all it craved for survival. Its instincts were compelled to the large human host. The creature was fulfilling its destiny. It was created to amalgamate with the higher conscious life form.

Dwanka's body temperature was almost depleted of warmth. In her comatose state, her will to fight was weakening as time passed. Deprivation of warmth and nutrition was too great for her body to overcome. The creature, a freak of nature, began swimming in the swampy water toward Dwanka. The creature's scaly body crawled out of the water. It headed up the mound stopping near its semi-conscious prey. Dwanka had sunk into an even lower state of dormancy. The reptile's body began to change colors. An illuminated, chromatic, spectrum of colors cascaded through the creature's body. As the living entity's mouth opened, a lengthy, pink tongue ejected from the body at an alarming velocity. It touched Dwanka's bare leg. Upon contact, the creature's outer hue changed to the exact color as that of Dwanka's skin tone. It was now in union with her. A unification that allowed the living entity to experience her emotional and physical state of being. The warmblooded creature continued toward its prey open-mouthed. The length of its tongue penetrated past her throat into her esophagus. The action afforded it a way to pass nutrition and other vital juices into Dwanka's body. The activity replenished her entire system, including her blood. As the copulation took place, something else phenomenally occurred. The creature transferred its life force into Dwanka. She had no knowledge of the biogenic transformation. When the transfusion was complete, the sacrificial exchange of life for a life allowed the chameleon to dissipate into nothingness. The purpose of its soul existence was completed.

Unaware of the great phenomenon that occurred, Dwanka suddenly awoke with a start. She opened her eyes feeling a strange sensation. She no longer was hungry or exhausted. She felt superbly energized. Dwanka noticed her senses were keener, her eyesight sharper, her hearing more heightened. She suddenly took heed to a strange taste that lingered on her tongue. Surprisingly, she stood feeling confidence to survival. Dwanka began moving onward toward her destination.

6.

Dwanka had now been traveling for hours in the daylight, it was something that she wouldn't have done earlier. She followed a river for the most part of the day. She walked feeling apprehensive about her surroundings.

Suddenly, noise erupted from the left near an undergrowth. Four men appeared from behind the dense forestry. They were trappers. The group were out hunting for whatever would bring them bounty. Dwanka remained still near a tree. Her heart rate soared from fear. The men neared. She noticed they wore strange clothing. The garments were nothing she'd ever witnessed. They created noise from laughter. The trappers were carrying rifles along with beige, burlap sacks on their backs. They were heading in her direction.

Dwanka remained quiet and motionless. Her heart felt as if it would jump out of her body. She thought her heartbeat was audile and would alert the trappers to her location. Dwanka began formulating an escape, a contingency plan if necessary. The trappers were two feet from her location. They stopped and began lighting cigarettes. The pungent odor enticed her to cough. She fought the urge because it would have exposed her location. A strange phenomenon entered her mind. Something within had also changed. A realization occurred to Dwanka. *'They don't see me.'*

The men talked for a while. Soon, they began moving onward. No attention was paid to her. Suddenly, one of the men stopped abruptly as if startled. He poised his body as if listening to a sound that was unfamiliar. Dwanka braced herself closer to the tree. *'This is it.'*

"What is it Rex?" asked a trapper. He discontinued his stride to look back at his friend. Rex remained still. He tried to pinpoint the location of the sound that only he heard.

"Ah its nuthin'. I thought I heard somethin' over there." He gestured by pointing his finger in the direction he referred to. "Somethin's strange. I felt a presence of bein' watched."

"That's all the coffee you've consumed lately." Laughter ensued.

"I guess you're right." He continued forward hurrying to catch up with the others.

Dwanka remained still. She didn't realize what had transpired. *'It's as if I were invisible.'* Unaware of the transformation, Dwanka's body had mutated along with the huge spruce tree she had taken refuge next to. Her body chemistry interchanged with the tree's molecular structure.

Dwanka's body held the ability to mimic all life forms. This was done involuntarily, she didn't know how it was executed. She could not control what was happening. She didn't feel any sensation when it was transpiring, nor did she have any remembrance of it.

All was now quiet again. The transformation to her former self was unfelt or forewarned. Dwanka continued onward by way of the Red River, which ended in Louisiana.

***

A clearing came into view in the dense forest. Dwanka had been on her trek for days. She was now able to survive on certain insects she came into contact with. She didn't understand how she came to crave such things. She developed an instinct for such a diet. Dwanka realized something was different about herself, only she couldn't comprehend any of it.

Peeking through underbrush, Dwanka spotted a small village. From her location she saw numerous huts in the center of a settlement. They were made from shrubs and vines. She witnessed people dressed in leafy garments. Their skin hues were tan and brown. She also noticed their hair was long, black, and silky. Dwanka read about the existence of such people. She remembered them being referred to as Native Indians. A fire burned in the center of the village. White smoke ascended toward the heavens as trees filtered some of the aroma. She saw women moving and tending to an open fire as they cooked and prepared food. To the left she saw children playing along side a stream. Dwanka gazed on intrigued. She didn't feel threatened by them. Food and rest is what she craved. She contemplated on her next move. Building confidence and courage, she headed toward the village.

FIVE

MONTHS

LATER

7.

Dwanka was accepted by the Chitimacha Indian tribal people. Other slaves had escaped their captors and taken refuge there. To Dwanka's surprise, the Africans spoke the native's language fluently. Most of the dialect used gestural motions and symbols. To her amazement, Dwanka learned the way of the Chitimacha people quickly. Lots of empathy was displayed by the Indians toward her.

From the time of the European invasion, the Chitmacha's population had dwindled tremendously. It was due to the wars and the foreign infections their bodies never built up a tolerance for. Diseases such as measles, smallpox, and typhoid fever were the culprits of deaths to their people. Diseases as such were never encountered in their environment until the invasion of the foreigners.

Dwanka was astonished at the agriculture and architecture used for survival on the Bayou Teche, the 125 mile waterway in Louisiana. The huts were built from a foundation of wooded poles plastered with mud and palmetto leaves. The roofs were thatched with the use of palm leaves for shelter. Dwanka was intrigued at how well they survived away from so-called civilization. The Chitimacha's diet consisted of a variety of corn, beans, squash, and melons. The women gathered wild foods and nuts. The men hunted for games such as deer, turkey, fish, and alligator. Their planning abilities were sophisticated. They stored grain in elevated granaries to supplement the hunting and fishing during the winter climates.

Living along the waterways, the natives traveled up and down the river in canoes made from dugout cypress logs. The water vessels were designed to accommodated up to four people. At times, game would have to be transported from further places. To defend themselves against intruders, they developed the blow dart and the cane dart. The weapons were made from sugar canes. The Chitimacha Indians used fishbones as arrowheads. When the fishbones were scarce, they would use stone carved arrows. The villager's dress code complimented their habitat. The men were dressed in breechcloth that shrouded their waist to cover their loins. The women wore short skirts, some were topless. Sexuality wasn't an issue. Cohabitation was done through rites of passage. The family of the female would present gifts to the family of the male counterpart. This was done so the couple would have a head start at being self sufficient. What was intriguing to Dwanka was the use of tattoos as each design held a signifiant caste system.

Dwanka found herself caring for the children. It was no problem for her. It gave her relief and took her mind off of the past.

***

The midday sun was positioned directly above Dwanka and the children. They kept cool by playing in the river. Five children were in her care. The ages ranged from six to eleven. For that particular tribe, age was calculated by the rotations of the seasons. There were no documents of birth dates. The group was playing a game with an object made from compressed leaves and tied into a ball. It floated in the water. The game was equivalent to the game of tag. Water splashed about as the children enjoyed the joyous occasion. The sounds of their laughter permeated the area.

Unexpectedly, at 30 yards away, four alligators became restless on the river bank located on the other side of the group. The splashing of water caused the curious reptiles to investigate the disturbance. It had been hours since they last fed. Simultaneously, the creatures entered the water and headed in the direction of the calamity.

Before Dwanka was able to visually see the intruders, she'd sensed the danger. When the alligators were sighted, it was too late for her to retrieve the children and get them to safety. A strange sensation overcame her. Dwanka began feeling lightheaded; a warmth stirred within her stomach and began rising upward. The more the force ascended from within, the hotter the sensation was felt. She no longer was able to see the water. During the mayhem, she lost sight of the children. Blackness was omnipresent. Dwanka submerged her entire body under the mirky water. The children were unaware of the dangers that lurked, they continued at play. A metamorphosis had begun within Dwanka. Her body began changing into a gigantic reptile. Her skin became hard and scaly. The hue of her skin became dark green with brown splotches. Dwanka's new form was double the size of the adversaries. She attacked at lightning speed. Her jaws clamped down with vise-like strength ripping flesh and organs. The river water changed from a bluish-green to a deep crimson hue. The children became frightened at the sight of the sudden change. The massive reptile sensed another alligator's threatening presence heading toward the children. The defending creature had finished demolishing one of the alligators and was just about finished with the second one when an even more phenomenal event occurred. The tail of the reptile changed form. Its tip was sharp and pointed. While retaining a deadly bite on its prey, the massive reptile's tail extended in length and attacked the wandering alligator. The steel-like tail penetrated through the scaly skin of the alligator. It entered into the side of the predator. The last alligator sensed its own demise. Using the gap in the distance, the lone alligator escaped into the murky, red water.

With the eminent danger over, Dwanka's body began a chemical reconstruction on a molecular level. The occurrence was instantaneous. She didn't feel the transformation, nor could she recall any of it. The sound of the children screaming and rushing toward the river bank was urgent. Dwanka joined them making sure everyone was safely on shore. After everyone was calmed, they made their way back to the village.

8.

Time passed, Dwanka noticed differences about her body. In the morning, she would awake feeling nauseated and vomiting. Her stomach had begun to protrude. It was puzzling to her because she knew nothing of such conditions. She had seen other women in the village in the same condition. Only to her thinking it was a tribal disease. She never talked with anyone about how that kind of circumstance was spawned. Dwanka didn't know if it was something that she'd done or was it forbidden food consumed. She was a virgin, but she did notice how a few of the males looked at her in a strange way. However, she dismissed the curious thoughts from her mind.

The village medicine man examined Dwanka. She was diagnosed as being pregnant. The news devastated her. She remained in a mental state of bewilderment. The medicine man observed that she didn't understand what was said nor about her condition. He spent a large portion of the morning explaining life's many cycles to her. He too was puzzled during the examination. He had noticed she was a virgin. Her hymen was undisturbed. His intuition indicated that something supernatural was happening. He meditated to the spiritual gods for an answer. The news devastated Dwanka. The concept was unsettling. As a result, she spent much of her time alone in a reflective state of mind. Deep inside her cognizance, Dwanka knew that something strange was happening. Not having any knowledge of organized religion, her intuitiveness revealed something archetypal was occurring, something that was never witnessed. She couldn't tap into it. She hoped it was something the world could reckon with.

During the gestation process, Dwanka was made to eat well and exercise regularly. Much time went into meditation. Dwanka realized that nothing ordinary was happening to her. She braced herself for what was to come. There was no way for anyone to explain the stupendous occurrence.

***

The months passed peacefully. Everyone in the village joined in with helping Dwanka bring forth a heathy boy into the world. Dwanka didn't understand why the villagers regarded her childbirth as a sad moment. When asked about it, she was informed by an elder in his native tongue. "Giving birth is viewed as a negative energy. We believe that prior to being manifested on this plane, such things as emotions, wants, and needs don't exist. We merely are. So, being delivered to this physical plan is the beginning of suffering. At the same instance, we believe it is a gift to experience emotions that couldn't be obtained in the spiritual plane."

Dwanka contemplated on what was said. "Elder." Her voice was mild and respectful. The tone was relative to a child hearing about life for the first time. "I am scared and I don't understand the meaning of this child."

The elder was adorned in animal cloth wrapped around his loins. Beads made from bear claws and alligator teeth were worn around his neck. He studied her for a moment before replying. Sweat glistened off of his bronze skin. "I witnessed in a dream the greatness you possess. You are endowed with an advance spiritual nature. In the vision, I have witnessed what you are capable of doing. Do not fret, your spirit will be passed onto your son. His name will be Awa. He will possess a greater power than you, more powerful than you could ever imagine. His name refers to the god of the seas and land."

Dwanka suddenly felt drained by the contents of the subject. "I feel tired, I think I will lie down. Thank you for everything."

***

Four years passed, Dwanka enjoyed bonding with Awa. He was a spitting image of his mother. The only distinctive difference in his appearance were his eyes. His pupils were a color impossible to describe with words. They seemed to constantly change colors. Awa was an intelligent and energetic tyke. He displayed great interest in water and other land animals in his surroundings. Awa was very observant to things happening around him. His mind at that age acted as a sponge soaking up knowledge. He picked up information and retain to memory the slightest details with clarity.

Dwanka and Awa sat at the edge of the river bank skipping stones. Awa was impressed at how far his mother could skim them over the water. The stones would skip at least six or seven times before sinking to the riverbed.

"Mom, why is it that most of the kids talk proudly about their fathers? How come I don't know my dad? They say everyone has a dad. Where is mine?" His eyes displayed sullenness.

Dwanka placed the stone she was about to toss into the river onto the dirt and stone riverbank. She gave Awa her undivided attention. "Son, you need not be ashamed of your circumstances." Dwanka moved closer to her son. "You are special. You are not like the others in this village. You are destined for something much greater than any of them."

Awa looked into his mother's eyes with a bewildered expression. He was curious to know more of what she was talking about. "So, who is he?"

"You mean your father?"

"Yes."

Dwanka took in a deep inhalation of air. She dispelled it to clear her emotions. She wanted to explain to her son without giving cause for worry. "As I said, you were born differently than the others. You were born without a father. I know it sounds strange and that it is difficult for you to grasp but you will. You may have special traits about yourself like I do, only we can't allow anyone to know they exist. It is better to keep it secret for now. Others will not understand."

Suddenly, the sound of bushes rattled. The discordant noise of yelling erupted in the once peaceful and natural terrain. Dwanka and Awa were startled. Men wearing blue uniforms with brass buttons appeared from behind the brush. Evidently, they had been observing for a while. Pointing musket rifles and silver swords, the hunters rushed toward them. The invaders shouted in an incomprehensible language. The aggressive actions of the trappers made Dwanka become aware of the seriousness of the situation. She felt as if her past had finally caught up with her. Visions of her former captivity as a slave flooded her memories vividly. She would be made an example for the rest to be fearful and to dispel any thoughts of replicating her actions.

Taking Awa by the hand, Dwanka yanked him with much force. Awa landed in her arms. Carrying his little body, Dwanka headed toward the dense swampland. Unknown to her, the village once filled with Chitimacha women and children had been obliterated by the invaders. Dwanka could hear the invaders in their wake as they rushed toward them at a rapid pace. Dwanka continued running through the wet marshland. She could feel her son's tiny heartbeat. Holding him tight, she tried to think of a way out of the situation. There was no way she could allow Awa to grow up in captivity as she once had. She thought about taking to the water remembering that she possessed some certain traits. *"No, I must continue on land I don't know if Awa has the same ability.'* A loud blast sounded from behind. Dwanka heard something whisk by her left ear. She continued to run at top speed; she was being fueled by adrenalin. The sound of galloping horses echoed near a ridge. Although they were out of sight, Dwanka heard the animals snort in an effort to breath as they were being forced to run at full gallop. The riders were tunnel visioned on the capture of slaves for trade.

Dwanka knew she would rather die than to go back into captivity. *'My son will never become a slave.'* The weight of Awa began to burden her small frame. There was undergrowth in the distance. Dwanka made her way toward that area. Heavy brush and vines that led into a ravine. With Awa cradled in her embrace, Dwanka sat with him quietly and motionlessly. Seemingly, both of the their heartbeats were synchronized into one. It was all she could think of to do to elude the pursuers. Gasping for breath, Dwanka whispered into Awa's ear. "Now you listen. What is happening may be confusing to you, but the people that are chasing us are bad men. They want to take us to a place and make us work for them. If anything happens to me, I want you to go onward. Run and don't look back." She eyed him closely. "Do you hear me?" Awa didn't answer. He stared into his mother's eyes sensing fear. Dwanka shook his small body by his upper arms. The boy was evidently frightened. He was being forced to make a grown up decision. "Do you hear me?"

The sharp tone of the question released Awa from his panic-stricken state. His voice was edgy. "Y-yes, mommy." He nodded. Their eyes told a story without words.

More rattling noise erupted in the brush behind them. "Com' on."

Taking his little hand, she moved forward.

Awa stumbled over some fallen tree branches. His body rolled toward a slight gap in the landscape. Dwanka removed the obstacle so that she could rescue him from the shallow ditch. Unseen, a net shrouded her entire body and restricted her movements. She felt hands grabbing her. Dwanka's attention remained directed toward the safety of her son. She made a decision. Dwanka needed to take the trapper's attention away from Awa. She began thrashing in a frantic motion. It was all she could do in effort to free herself.

"Look Glenn, we've got ourselves a fighter." There were two trappers. They were both dressed in dirty, smelly, blue uniforms. Subconsciously, Awa took notice to the brass buttons that fastened the garment down the center. They wore dirty hats that resembled domes upon their heads. They were the same color as the uniforms.

"Yeah, she's a pretty one. Maybe we should sample the goods before we sell her." His voice was a deep baritone. "I hear they're good in the hay." He chuckled.

The two men began to manhandle Dwanka. She continued putting up a struggle. They removed the net cover from around her body. The two men began to handle her roughly. One held her arms behind her head in a full nelson hold, while the other man parted her legs in efforts to straddle her for sexual purposes. Dwanka fought with all her might. The men continued to overpower her with force. Tears streaming from her eyes. With the last ounce energy depleted, Dwanka surrendered to her attackers. *'I hope Awa is far away by now.'* She felt one of the men violently enter her.

Awa was riddled with fear and anger. The feelings he possessed overpowered his system. A new level of emotions surfaced. He experienced sensations he never knew existed. Bewilderment overwhelmed him. Awa was stunned and unable to move. The only control he possessed was his vision. It allowed him to watch what the men were doing to his mother. His mind absorbed the details. Vivid images were being burned into his psyche. His mind struggled to process the data. Watching it all unfold, something strange began working on a molecular level inside of his mind and body. Awa's mental fibers became infused with emotional and physical torment. He witnessed his mother being abused. He observed as she stopped thrashing defensively and accepted defeat. Dwanka lie listless, she no longer moved or breathed. The sight of the event changed his worldview forever. Awa felt helpless and afraid. He remained quiet in the entrenchment watching the men as they finished what they were doing to his mother. Afterward, they moved onward. Awa exited from his covering. He approached his mother who was naked and bruised. Her eyes were closed. She breathless and lifeless. He shook her in efforts to awaken her. He wanted them to continue on their journey. He loved the way she talked and told him stories. Awa tried to revive her. After the fruitless attempts, his mind began replaying her last instructions. *'If anything happens to me I want you to go on. Run! Don't look back. Do you hear me?'* His mind recalled the moment with clarity. The thought made him wipe the tears from his eyes and move forward into the evening. The sunset was already positioned across the horizon. A chromatic spectrum of colors illuminated the sky. Splotches of yellow, red, and orange were painted across the celestial. A dark, royal-purple sky took up the backdrop giving the scene a picturesque existence. Awa continued onward. Through teary eyes, he remained watchful and alert in the foreign wilderness. He traveled aimlessly in the nocturnal setting. Awa remembered what his mother told him about the Northern Star.

9.

The distressing past caused an identity crisis for Awa. At times things seemed confusing to him making it difficult to distinguish the past from the present. His body began to change. He began changing forms. His appetite was also peculiar.

Years passed, Awa went by many different nomenclatures to describe who he was. During his body changes, he used the outer skin from others. He noticed every time the transformation happened his attitude changed. His worldview was drastically distorted. Awa developed a deep-seated dislike for uniformed, authority figures. Memories of his mother dissipated with time, but hurt and hatred developed from witnessing the abuse she sustained. Something struck his persona in a twisted way after witnessing the sexual attack on his mother. He was intrigued with the aspect of how the men felt when the act was being committed. At times he would be engrossed with rage at the thought of how she was mishandled. The mixed emotions were impossible for him to separate.

A strange occurrence was noticed. Over the decades, Awa had become aware he didn't age physically. For a person 72 years old, he looked as if he were in his late twenties. Another oddity existed. His diet changed drastically. He no longer craved insects that sustained him in the past. His tastebuds now craved human blood. Awa developed a deep-seated need for sex. It was an urge beyond the level of lust. It was more like a seasonal mating fury, only seasons had nothing to do with it. When the urge arise, it had to be fulfilled. During the encounter, his mind would visualize what the trappers had done to his mother. Inside his twisted cognizance, Awa felt he was avenging his mother's death through the sexual acts. Another event presented itself. Unlike the other predecessors of his kind, he was the most vicious of all the other species that had ever received the opportunity to morph into what he now was. There were millions of creatures walking on all fours awaiting the god-like change he had been endowed with. During his molecular reconstruction transformation period, he grew the same extremities his ancestors possessed. With the use of his unnaturally, lengthy fingernails, he was able to shed the skin of his prey without damage. He would adorn their epidermis over his own body seamlessly.

Awa drifted along the Red River for decades stopping along the way to feed on campers. The insatiable urge to feed became great. His thirst for women intensified as time passed. With less adversaries left to contend with, Awa traveled toward the inland. Traveling at night he found himself in a township called Shottenville. It was a small county with a main street that housed shops along both sides of a narrow throughway. Everything was serene and quiet. Awa traveled on a back road. A high school came into view. A large marquee read 'Ridge Mount High School. Home of Shottenville's Warheads'. The sign signified the team was number one in the conference finals. A large football field was located in the rear. Awa headed aimlessly through the quiet back roads. Approximately a mile along a dark roadway, Awa saw a huge patch of land. An aged, handmade sign with years of sun faded ink was held in place by rusty nails on a cypress tree. The wood itself was splintered and weather beaten. It read 'Old Man Cutter's Cornfield'. Although it was dark, the sunrise was about to perform its miracle of illuminating the sky. Cautiously, Awa looked in both directions before proceeding. The cornfield seemed endless. Awa knew he could survive at that location indefinitely.

SEVEN

MONTHS

LATER

10.

Officer Wainwright was summoned to the coroner's office. He sat in the office of Mr Clanton, a second generation pathologist. Mr Clanton was a tall, slender, man with a well kept beard and goatee. His eyeballs protruded from their sockets giving him a sleepy appearance.

"I called for you because I know this case is personal to you." He retrieved some documents from a file folder. "Okay, the jelly mass discovered in the cornfield actually are the internal organs belonging to Sonny Larks. DNA has confirmed that. From the coagulation period and the discoloration settings we were able to determine the time of death a ten hour window. The mystery is the skin was removed from the body in an advanced way. A method we have no knowledge about. Somehow, the skin tissue is all that is missing from the cadaver."

"What could have done something so heinous? It's horrific to say the least. We've never had anything horrible as this in the town's entire history. How can you be so sure as to how long Sonny's body was there?"

"We used the Potassium Eye Fluid Test." He noticed Officer Wainwright's facial expression displayed bafflement. "You see, when a person is alive there is very little build up in the eyes. At death, the red blood cells break down and the potassium enters the vitreous fluids very slowly. This level rises predictably. We can estimate a time frame from that alone."

"Okay, I understand." Officer Wainwright studied the file folder in front of him. "This substance found at the scene, have you found a match?"

"Actually we have. We've cross-matched it but it doesn't make any sense to us."

"What do you mean?"

"We've matched it to that of a chameleon. Like I said, it doesn't make sense. Those creatures are harmless to humans.

"I spoke with my daughter and she swears what she heard was a sound not like anything she'd ever heard. This thing raped my little girl. Mind you, we are from a faith that doesn't allow abortions." Officer Wainwright covered his face with his hands. Frustration mounted heavily in his psyche.

Mr Clanton touched him on the shoulder. "I understand. Maybe soon we'll get more clues to this strange phenomenon."

"I hope you're right."

***

Officer Wainwright entered the house. Customarily, he placed his keys on the table and headed directly upstairs to his bedroom. It was midday and sunlight filtered into the room through the open blinds. He undressed, placing on a pair of comfortable blue jeans. He always showered after leaving work. Officer Wainwright heard a noise stemming from down the hall. Curiosity won him over, he went to investigate. The room down the hall belonged to Amber. He knocked subtly.

"Com' in."

Sticking only his head through the threshold, Officer Wainwright peered in at his daughter. "Feel like talking for a spell?"

"Sure dad, come in." Amber watched her father enter the room. She tried to read his demeanor. "Did you find anything of importance?"

Her father sat down in a chair next to the bed. "The autopsy revealed the remains were Sonny's." The information jolted her as if she had been hit by an unseen object. He comforted her with an embrace. "The mystery is the DNA of the substance found in you is said not be earthly. The forensic team said it was cross-matched with a chameleon. I don't understand it either but if you accept to abort I will understand."

Amber stood quickly. "You may." Tears clouded her vision. "What about God? Do you think that He would forgive me for taking a life? Suppose I have the only child that will find the cure for Aids or world hunger and I killed all the possibilities just to satisfy my own selfish need." Amber wiped at her tear-soaked face. "No, I don't think that I could ever live with that responsibility, or should I say that kind of guilt."

Her father stood making eye contact with her. "It's your decision. I am with you. Anything that you decide, I am here for you." He headed out of the door.

11.

Amber Wainwright found herself in a contemplative state. She thought about the reason why things had to be the way they were. She missed Sonny dearly. Since the horrid ordeal with Sonny, she found herself constantly thinking about him. Everything reminded her of him. It had been a depressing seven months. Amber felt her body going through an unfamiliar cycle. The sensations were foreign to her. She'd never experienced pregnancy, not knowing if it was the normal or not. *'I hope all this anxiety I am feeling isn't affecting my baby.'* Amber decided to continue with her last year in high school.

Today, she sat in the public library across from her girlfriend Melanie. Melanie was an African-American girl that attended the same high school. She was Amber's confidant. When Sonny and her began dating, their union became the talk of the town. Interracial relationships were frowned upon in Shottenville. It was Melanie that persuaded Amber to follow her own heart no matter what others thought. Amber adhered to the advice acknowledging that Melanie was correct in her assumption that love conquers all. Even now she didn't regret having the baby. She had no one to fault. Her main misfortune was the baby wasn't Sonny's offspring. Feeling sacrilegious, Amber relied on the belief she was experiencing a supernatural phenomenon.

"Melanie I'm scared." The outburst was conveyed unexpectedly. Amber quietly closed the textbook she was studying from.

Melanie was taken aback by the sudden eruption. Melanie was a pretty girl with plain features. Her dark complexion and pouty lips were glamorous. Guys found her appearance seductive. She reached for Amber's hand to comfort her. "It's natural to feel that way. You will get through this. Just know I'll be there for you every step of the way."

"Thank you I…" Amber's attention was adverted suddenly toward a large showcase window in the shop. She stared out toward an object. The showcase window was positioned toward the street side of the entrance.

"What is it?"

Amber's attention was returned. There was enthusiasm in her voice. "Mel you might think I am crazy but everything reminds me of Sonny. Once, he was seemingly the only one in town with a red pickup truck. I now see them all the time. It makes me jittery."

"That isn't crazy. I understand. How about we get an ice cream float? I need a break. My eyes are beginning to cross from looking at all these numbers." The sound of laughter ensued from the pair.

Walking down Main Street, Amber and Melanie were conversing joyously. Suddenly, Amber stopped in stride. She stared at an object across the street. Her focus was undivided on an unfamiliar location.

"What is it now Amber? You know this has to stop." Melanie looked at her friend with uncertainty.

"Look! Over there!" Her index finger was extended toward people walking on the other side of the street. Cars moved along on the two-way street.

"What are you pointing at?" Melanie was puzzled. She scanned in the direction that was mentioned.

"That's Sonny!" Amber's voice was heightened with excitement. "The guy with the black hoodie and black jeans."

Melanie looked in the direction that was mentioned. Across the street was a busy scene. Melanie spotted the back of the person wearing what Amber described. "Look, Amber that's enough. You have to get over this. Sonny is gone. There are official police documents claiming it. I know it's hard when you lose someone you love. You have to accept it so that you can move forward. Being in denial is just going to make matters worse." Melanie studied her friend. She felt remorseful after the reprimand. "Let's get you home. Today was a long day."

Amber entered the house feeling sad and drained. Her father was in the kitchen going over some documents from work. He looked up from the heap of paperwork on the table to see his daughter entering. He noticed her presence displayed a mirthless demeanor.

"Hey Pumpkin, what is it?" He knew she'd been under a lot of stress lately. "How did the studying go at the library? Did you get a lot accomplished?" Amber was entranced in deep thought. She didn't acknowledge a word her father had spoken. Instead, she headed directly to her room.

Entering the room, she flopped on the bed and began sobbing. Soon a knock came on the door. Not hearing a reply, her father placed his ear to the door. He heard whimpering on the other side. Mr Wainwright slowly turned the doorknob. He inched the door open enough to see if his little girl was properly dressed. He saw her on the bed sobbing. Although it had been months since the tragic incident, he knew Amber had been mentally reliving the ordeal immensely. *'Maybe I should make an appointment to see Dr Westler.'* He pretended to cough as he entered the room. It was a feigned effort to make his presence known. "Babe, I don't mean to upset you any further or pry. It's just I am worried about you. Are you sure you want to go on with this pregnancy? You know you don't have to prove any point with anyone."

Amber looked to her father with reddened eyes. "I know dad." She wiped at her tearful eyes. "The entire ordeal is so bizarre. Sometimes, I think it could be an abomination. You raised me to respect all life and that is instilled inside of me. How can I even think to abort?"

"I know it's a tough decision you are stuck with. I just want you to know I am with you every step of the way."

"I know dad, thank you." She raised from her position and gave her father an empathetic embrace and kiss on the cheek.

The emotions also brought moisture to his eyes. "Okay." He sighed. Feeling uncomfortable, he tried to change the subject.

"Dinner will be ready in an hour. Get ready."

"Okay, I won't be late dad."

12.

Awa was confused with his ability to extract the skin of other males and adorn it. The trait was naturally bestowed upon him; it wasn't a studied craft. Incomprehensibly, it was something integrated into his being. His craving for food and sex heightened. It wasn't a lustful nor gluttonous kind of desire. He probed his surroundings looking for prey. Not knowing any other way of life, Awa didn't know if what he was experiencing was natural. Although the desires weren't constant, they did existed. At times he could go extended periods in between urges. His desires were separated. It was either the need for sex or for nourishment. The feelings were never simultaneous. Tonight it was for mating.

Wearing Sonny's epidermis, he canvassed the small town's limited resources. The only hindrance was he couldn't speak while wearing the outer layer. He spotted a woman standing outside an establishment; she was alone. As he neared, he noticed she was smoking a cigarette. The establishment she stood in front of was a poolroom. She wore a short, gray skirt that was hiked to her thighs. The outfit exposed flesh. She adorned a belly shirt that allowed view of her well toned stomach. Her navel was pierced with a shimmering stud. The streets were quiet and barren of pedestrian traffic. A few cars passed from time to time. The temperature was mild; the wind blew a gentle breeze from the Gulf. Stars twinkled in the nocturnal sky. From that distance, Awa was able to sense the woman's biochemical makeup. Strangely, he was aware she was at the point of ovulation. It was a ravishing scent that was relevant to the mating call in the wild. It drove him fervidly wild. Awa hungered for the feeling of release. He sensed his prey. In his cognizance, it was exactly what his mother experienced before her untimely death. He walked on the quiet deserted sidewalk with his hands in his pocket. His hooded sweatshirt covered his head. Awa passed in front of the woman without saying a word.

"Hey! Where are you going? Are you looking for some action?" Her southern accent carried a guttural tone. She tossed a cigarette she held to the ground. There was very little white paper left. Awa stopped his stride and gaze at her. He couldn't speak because of the skin covering. He continued gazing. "Oh, you're one of those silent types, huh?" She neared to get a good look. She liked what she saw. "I'll tell you what honey, for 50 bucks we don't have to talk. I like the silent type anyway." She chuckled.

Awa only nodded. She led him around the corner to a boarding house. He paid the fee for the room and paid her for service. Awa used the currency found in the teen's pocket when he'd overtaken him in the cornfield. They were given a key to a room.

Before completely clearing the threshold and closing the door, the woman was already stripping off her clothes. She even helped Awa undo his own clothing. The urge rekindled. Uncontrollably, Awa became the aggressor. A wild animalistic lust was displayed in his love making. She'd never felt anything like it. It was a disturbing sensation. She began enjoying the pleasure. *'I should be paying him for this.'* The thought amused her. Before she realized, she was unconscious.

The woman awoke disconcerted. Momentarily she was unable to recall her whereabouts or what led her to being there. She smiled as the memories returned. Suddenly, everything changed. A chilling scream escaped her lips. It was a deafening shriek; a terrifying cry from fear. She looked upon the bed unable to comprehend what she saw. The unidentified substance was gross. Adjacent to her on the bed was a layer of skin. The epidermis was in the formation of a human body with no internal organs. She noticed a sticky substance covered her body.

***

The woman sat in the precinct across from Officer Wainwright. The office space was cramped and cluttered with file cabinets and shelves holding boxes and dusty files. His desktop was littered with documents. Officer Wainwright remembered the woman in front of him. He had brought her in for prostitution a few times in the past. Other than that, he knew she was harmless. Today she looked disheveled. Her hair was in disarray and her clothes were soiled. He noticed her nervous expression.

"So, you're saying this person actually raped you?" A smirked appeared on his face. "You do know that if you received payment it isn't considered rape."

"I know it doesn't look good on my part because of my profession. That is understood. What I am saying is whatever it was that I was with wasn't human. I mean he looked human. You saw what was left on the bed. I need to be examined to see what kind of disease that thing has given me."

"Okay, we can do that. Can you describe him?"

"Yes,"

"Good." Officer Wainwright picked up the telephone and dialed. He adverted his attention to the receiver and the person on the other end of the line. "Berton we need a perp-sketch done. We're on our way there." He replaced the receiver on the cradle.

A digital computer facial profile was designed using the information that was provided by the woman. Officer Wainwright studied the image. It looked familiar to him, yet he couldn't place a name to the face. So much was going on in his life that certain skills he prided himself with in the past were marred. A thought occurred as he picked up the telephone and dialed. "It's me, did anything turn up? Okay, I'm on my way."

Back at the forensic laboratory, Molly Fenson waved Officer

Wainwright over. She was standing at her station. It was adjacent to a table that held an assortment of testing equipment and microscopes.

"You won't believe this, substance found on that woman is the same as that in the cornfield. Still, it's very much a mystery and untraceable with the technology we have. We've sent the last samples to Washington. Hopefully, they've found something by now."

"How about the substance found on the bed?"

"That is the bizarre part. After doing a thorough analysis, we've found that it it the exact DNA of the deceased boy Sonny."

"But how can that be?"

"We don't understand it neither. We do know the test is accurate."

Officer Wainwright snapped his finger as an idea occurred. "Molly thanks, I have to go." He hurried out of the door.

Molly Fenson looked on bewildered as Officer Wainwright's demeanor abruptly changed to an urgent mode. She shrugged her shoulders dismissing the thought. She adverted her attention to the work at hand.

Officer Wainwright entered the hospital in search for the woman that was admitted for testing. He entered the room. She was in bed. All test had been completed. The test concluded with most of the diagnosis being psychological. They were also concerned about any contaminants of a contagious viral disease like Ebola. Officer Wainwright carried a manilla envelope.

"I want to show you something." He removed a large eight by ten inch color photograph from the envelope. He showed it to her. "Is this the guy you were with last night?"

The woman viewed the photograph. Her eyes widened as she recognized the image. "Yes, that's him. That's him!" There was excitement in her voice.

Officer Wainwright stood. "Thank you." He retrieved the photograph from the woman then exited the room.

Officer Wainwright went directly home. He headed directly toward Amber's room. He knocked on the door.

"Com' in."

"I don't mean to disturb you but I need to ask you something. You said you saw Sonny yesterday on the streets. What was he wearing?"

"Black hooded sweatshirt and black jeans. Why?"

"Baby you are not crazy. Someone else spotted him also. I don't know what is going on but we'll get to the bottom of this."

13.

Awa needed to find a body fast. Always after a sexual encounter, he needed to change skin. He would have used the woman's epidermis, only females weren't physically suited for him. Women's bodies were uninhabitable. For that reason all his slaughtered victims were males. One species was for lust, the other was for transporting himself in society.

Awa came across a Seven-Eleven convenience store. A single gas pump island was in front of the store. A vehicle recently pulled away from the pump after refueling. Awa approached. His eyes were multi-pivotal with independent movement. He scanned his surroundings. The area quiet; the only person around was the attendant. The clerk was adorned in uniform. He was an elderly man in his mid 50's. Salt and pepper colored hair covered his head. His face was clean shaven.

The attendant's skin held blotches of discolored, reddish spots.

Awa entered the store. He headed directly toward the beverage section. A low audio of instrumental music played mildly on the overhead public address system. The sound gave ambience to the shopping experience. Retrieving a bottle of water, Awa twisted the cap off bottle and turned it up to his mouth. Awa guzzled the entire content from the plastic bottle in a single gulp.

The conversion always made him thirsty. He tossed the bottle to the floor and retrieved another. The clerk took notice and left from behind the counter. He approached the man from behind and tapped the customer on the shoulder.

"Excuse me sir, drinking in the store prohibited."

Awa turned around to face the clerk. The exposure of his green, scaly skin was visible. His skin texture was fully reptilian. His eyes were slitted and the eyelids blinked from side to side. It was nothing the clerk ever witnessed. The clerk stood completely bewilderment and in shock. Fear overwhelmed his emotions. The clerk's mouth was gaped. He experienced a sharp pain. Shock medicated his body from the total sensation. The experienced was short lived. Blankness overcame him. All existence as he once knew ceased forever.

Three patrol cars were parked in front of the Seven-Eleven convenience store at different angles. The vehicle's emergency lights illuminated the area, flashing red and blue. Inside the store were three uniformed officers. Officer Wainwright was one of them. The scene was gruesome. There were organs, bile, blood, and body fluids strewn about the back of the store. The officers wore latex gloves. They tried to get a handle on the situation. They had been notified by an anonymous caller who had stopped to purchase gas.

Moments later, the forensic team arrived. Molly Fenson entered the store wearing powder-blue, latex gloves. She adorned a white, laboratory coat. Her crew went into action. They began taking pictures throughout the store. Officer Wainwright approached her.

"You don't have to say it. Yes, it's the same pattern."

"Let me guess…no one witnessed anything. Right?"

"Right!" retorted Officer Wainwright. A thought occurred.

Snap!

It was an animate sound of his fingers reacting to his thought. He turned on his heels. "That's it!" Molly Fenson gazed at him perplexed. She was baffled to his meaning. It dawned on her when he pointed toward the surveillance camera overhead. It was located at the front of the store.

A smile occurred on his face. He adverted his attention to another officer. "See if you can find the tape from the camera. Maybe there's something on it that will help explain this." Officer Wainwright gazed out of the large, glass window toward the street side to see a local news truck had arrived. "Get someone out there to block them from entering. We don't need anyone interfering with the crime scene."

The precinct was busy. A buzz of excitement filled the air. Shottenville has never experienced the trouble it faced. The talk of the town was about Sonny being killed. Amber's name was associated with the story. It was rumored she had been raped by Sonny and was now pregnant. With the news report about the Seven Eleven murder, everyone in town was apprehensive. The fear of a killer at large was overwhelming.

"I can't believe what I am seeing. If I didn't know better I would've thought special effects were implemented here. How can this be?" Officer Wainwright sat viewing the videotape from the Seven Eleven surveillance camera with other officers.

"What are we looking at?" asked Officer Hal.

"Looks like something from another planet," responded another officer.

Officer Wainwright became worried about Amber and her state of mind. *'I can't allow her to have that baby. Not at any cost.'*

14.

Officer Wainwright walked into the house angered over the information he'd received. He knew there was no way he would allow Amber to go forward with her pregnancy. Amber was in her bedroom studying. She was also scanning the website for instructions on pregnancy preparations. Her father walked into the room ranting about an abortion. The conversation took a negative turn quickly.

"Even if I wanted to it's too late now. I am into term. I am seven months in." She stood to show her growing baby bump to her father. She looked wonderful in motherhood. Her physical features were at full blossom. He kept his mind on what he'd witnessed on the video tape from the Seven Eleven convenience store.

"There has to be something that can be done. You can't go on with this. It will ruin you once it goes wrong."

Amber interjected. "You don't know that for sure."

"I know what I saw. Okay, I was trying to spare you the initial shock of discovery. Since you insist, put on your clothes you're coming with me. I want to show you something."

***

At the precinct, Amber viewed the videotape from the surveillance camera at the Seven-Eleven convenience store. She watched in pure amazement. Skepticism entered her being.

"How do you know that's inside me? You don't know for sure what happened with me other than me being raped. No! I won't do it!" Amber stood abruptly. She rushed from the building in tears. Her father slammed his fist on the desk as frustration mounted within. He didn't chase after her. He wanted her to take in the full effect of her choice.

Amber was now in a ball of mass confusion. She understood her father's concerns, but she wasn't going to abort the life growing inside of her. *'I can't! There would be no forgiveness if I'm wrong.'* Amber hurried home with an agenda in mind.

She began packing a few necessities. She rushed to the bank before closing and retrieved her entire savings. Amber found herself on a Greyhound bus heading toward the northern region of New York. The brochure she received from the bus depot read 'New

York City'. Prior to boarding the bus, she purposely trampled on her cellphone. She discarded the crushed, electronic parts into a trash receptacle. Amber wanted no contact with her past.

***

Meredith Wainwright had just returned from a cosmetic convention in Chicago. She entered the house. Throughout the time spent from home, she worried about her daughter. She felt an uncertainty as to what was becoming of her family. She called out to Amber in the quiet house. There was no reply. She entered Amber's room to find it vacant. Something odd captured her attention. Normally, Amber's room would be in pristine condition. Now items were strewn about. She headed from the room to get dinner prepared. Meredith knew she had to bring normalcy back to the household. During the task of cooking, her husband entered. Their eyes grew in pure amazement and delight.

"When did you get in? Why didn't you call? I would have picked you up."

"I wanted to surprise you with a good dinner. I know that you two have been eating takeout since my departure. So, I figured we'll get back to normal." She was at the cubbyhole retrieving some spices. "I didn't see Amber. Where is she?"

"I thought she would have been here by now. I had another conversation with her about aborting the pregnancy. I showed her the evidence of some bizarre happening that may be related to her condition."

"Are you absolutely sure about the proof?"

He was hesitant for a moment. "No, not exactly. I just think it will damage her life even before it begins."

"Yes, but overall it's her choice. Remember we raised her that way. To respect life."

"This is different. We don't know who's responsible for her pregnancy. If it's what I think it is, she'll thank me later."

"Okay, get ready. Dinner will be served shortly. Go wash up. I'll call her."

15.

Amber had been on her road trip for almost an entire day. After leaving Louisiana, she passed through Texas which is the largest state in the country. A lot of raw emotions streamed through her. Her mind was constantly shifting thoughts about her predicament. She felt the baby stir inside her womb. The scar on her side tingled as it was beginning to heal. She rubbed it as a constant reminder. It was one of the tell-tale signs to signify she'd been raped. She reflected on her father's concerns and what her decision would do to her already devastated mother. The lost of Sonny was the core of her sadness.

After two long days on the road, Amber found herself in New York City. It was a place she'd only read about. Compared to Shottenville, it was a huge city with more people moving about than she'd ever could imagined. She stood in the famous Times Square Center. In the past, Amber had watched the ball drop on television from the same area on New Years's Eve celebrations. She never thought she would be there physically. She remembered viewing thousands of people that has stood in the same area. She studied her surroundings as people walked by without saying a word, nor giving notice that she existed.

The temperature was much colder than in Shottenville. She picked up on the social disassociation of the people. Everyone seemed to be preoccupied with their own thoughts. Unlike in her hometown where people were friendly. Her first stop was to find an affordable jacket.

Amber entered into a shop on a side street. The clerk sized her, selling her a dark blue, windbreaker jacket. Exiting the store with her knapsack strapped to her shoulder, she went in search for a place to eat.

Sitting inside a quaint eatery, Amber found the food delicious. When the bill arrived she was stunned. *'Wow! Everything in this city is so expensive. My little funds will be gone in no time if I stay here.'* Amber noticed a woman watching her periodically. She was located at a table adjacent from where she sat. She smiled when their eyes met.

"I'm sorry for staring. I was just noticing your pregnancy and that you're such a lovely girl."

"Thank you. I was just admiring the prices in this town. Is everything so expensive?"

The woman was in her mid 50's. Her features were plain. She wore stylish clothing along with dainty jewelry. "You're not from here, are you?"

Amber looked on sheepishly. "Is it that obvious?"

The woman waved it off. "Not quite, we New Yorkers are so immune to the high prices we don't think about it."

"How is it that people can afford them? Where I'm from the wages couldn't meet these demands."

The woman chuckled. "Where are you from?"

"Shottenville, Louisiana."

The woman rubbed her chin as a quizzical thought emerged. "Oh, I see."

"It's a really small town along the Red River."

"So, what are you doing so far away from home?"

Amber stood. "May I?" She gestured to sit at the stranger's table.

"Sure." Her smile was delightful.

Amber sat with the pretty woman. "My name is Amber." She outstretched her hand.

"My name is Gertrude, my friends call me Gert. You can call me Gert." She received Amber's hand.

"Well, I'm here to have my baby."

"Where's the father, if you don't mind me asking? Why isn't he here?"

Amber looked away feeling self-conscious. It still was an emotional topic. "My boyfriend died trying to protect me."

"I don't mean to pry but may I ask from what?"

"They don't know who killed him but whoever it was raped me in the process. See, I was unconscious and I don't believe in abortions. My family doesn't approve of my decision. So here I am." She sighed deeply. "There I said it."

Gertrude sensed the struggle it took for Amber to confide in her. She looked at Amber, then the food on her plate. She used that time to make a hasty decision. "Since you don't have anywhere to go, you're coming with me. New York isn't a place for a young, beautiful runaway such as yourself. I won't accept no for an answer." The woman gestured for the checks.

FIVE

MONTHS

LATER

16.

Awa moved about aimlessly. Time passed purposefully. As the months passed, his sexual urges were lessened. It was as if his body knew a change was coming, a closing of an old era and the opening of a new frontier. Awa moved instinctively, nothing was thought out or planned. He existed to be who he was. He held natural insight knowing he was there to serve a purpose, to fulfill a legacy. His mission was to make sure his lineage survived the transitional period. Awa felt his life ebbing away. He yearned to be at a familiar place. It was at that moment he began his trek.

Amber stayed in the lavish home that belonged to Gertrude Pemberton. It was located in a posh section in Long Island. The house was an Old Georgian designed home with lots of space and history. Original window shutters were well kept. Amber discovered that Gertrude was a wealthy widow. Her husband had owned a Fortune 500 company in the retail industry. She was barren and never adopted any children. She lived a lavish lifestyle that she'd grown accustomed to. Now, she lived with regrets because life without Wilfred, her deceased husband, was lonely and purposeless. Meeting Amber was a godsend, a breath of fresh air. She would do anything and everything in her power to bring Amber comfort and security. Amber had never lived in a house so humongous. Maids and servants visited during the day. It was Gertrude's way of making the house seemed lived in. The staff was viewed as her informal family. Most of the 14 rooms in the house went unused. Gertrude looked forward to the new energy Amber and her soon-to-be child would bring to the house. Amber went into labor in the evening. She was rushed to a private hospital nearby.

"Push! One more time. You're doing fine. You are crowning nicely," encouraged the head nurse. In the cozy hospital, Amber was being given royal treatment. Her vital signs were closely monitored. Another nurse dabbed her forehead with a cotton pad. Gertrude waited in a designated area for the ordeal to be over.

Two hours later, a doctor wearing lime-green scrubs, along with a face mask pulled down near his chin, approached Gertrude. He was her personal physician. The doctor had changed his entire scheduling to do her this favor of performing the delivery for Amber.

"It is done. It's a healthy baby boy. We are doing test to make sure everything is in order. They should be home in a few days if all goes well."

"Thank you Sam."

"You are very welcome."

At the exact moment the baby began emerging, Awa sat on the ground at the very site he'd witnessed his mother being sexually abused and murdered. Now, he would lie down next to her. He wanted to absorb the pain and torment she endured over seven decades ago. To him, it felt like yesterday. During the nonverbal conversation, he and his mother reunited. At that moment of finality, Awa rested his head on the dirt ground as he sensed his mother's energy. It was the same dirt that his mother touched saving his life and sacrificing her own in the process. A longing existed, a cycle was being met. Awa felt a coldness inside of his being. Suddenly, a relief of pressure was lifted from his body and mind. His true essence ebbed out of his body. It rose toward a fading cloud. It traveled faster than the speed of light toward a new destination. It was the same process done to the others before him. Each predecessor evolved in a different manner, all moving toward a supreme manifestation. Suddenly, Awa's body was no more. His body dematerialized. His purpose was fulfilled.

17.

At the moment of birth, a supreme energy permeated the body of the newborn. The force was so great it energized all of the major organs in the body to excel in growth. The sensory instincts were heightened beyond that of any human being. He cried aloud at the start of his life. The sudden yelp associated with mortal babies upon emergence was different, this cry was similar to pent up frustration, anger, and sadness. It was a continuance of the emotions associated with his ancestors.

He was named Sonny. Amber knew the child didn't belong to him but the wishful thought was there. The memory of the incident was attached to him. Gertrude took Amber in. She made sure they were taken care of. The instant awareness of Sonny not resembling the mother didn't matter; he brought life back into Gertrude's existence.

Staff was hired to tend to Amber's needs. Amber and Gertrude sat in the kitchen eating breakfast.

"I don't know how to keep saying thank you, although I will learn. You have been a true blessing to me and my son. I don't think I could have made it this far without you. You've never once judged me about my past."

"Child you don't have to thank me. I feel we saved one another. I love having you both here. As you can see there is plenty of room." She gestured with her hands.

Time passed gracefully, Amber matured wisely while raising Sonny. Sometimes she would watch him at play and wonder how he would have looked if he were truly Sonny's offspring. He didn't resemble her in the least. If known any better, she would have thought a switch had taken place at the hospital. Amber's skin was pale, Sonny's hue was slightly tan with an olive sheen. Her eyes were almond shaped, his were oval. Her hair was blonde, his the same.

Sonny was a lively and happy baby. He was healthy and affectionate. He displayed an endless supply of energy. It was very peculiar to see how fast Sonny's body was developing. Amber began using a ruler to record his height. She add the date and the time in an entry log book. His appetite was increasing as time passed. Witnessing the change, she wondered if her father's worries carried validity.

***

The Wainwrights did everything in their power to track Amber's whereabouts. No traces were found. The deployment of a national all-points-bulletin was useless in locating her. There were no activity of her social security number, or birth certificate being used at any institution in the United States. It baffled him to know how she could be sustaining herself this long without support. There were no family they knew of that would keep her without notifying them.

As time passed, he blamed himself. Mr Wainwright and his wife found themselves arguing endlessly about Amber's reason for leaving so abruptly and taking their grandchild.

"We were too hard on her. She was scared and all you could do was push her to abort."

"If you would have witnessed what I saw you would understand why."

"We see what you've managed to do. Now she's gone." Tears streamed down her cheeks.

***

At age ten, Sonny tried out for his school's football team. For his age, he was more muscular and taller than the rest of the boys. Usually, in certain events, proof of his age was requested.

Gertrude took them to the Florida Keys. It was there they enjoyed the comforts of southern hospitality. Gertrude owned a cottage that was well kept while she was away. Her and her husband used the place during the winter months when they wanted to escape the northern frigid temperatures.

The land mass was spacious. The property faced the Gulf. A beautiful fiberglass boat, painted the color of pearl with metallic sparkles, scintillated when the sunlight reflected. It moored in front of the cottage. A short wooden pier gave access to water. The sounds of seagulls squealed above as they hovered in the clear, blue sky. Everything seemed picturesque. As soon as Amber spotted the jet ski moored next to the boat she wanted to ride.

Later that day, they ventured on the pathway called Gator's Cove. It was a path that led through the swampland. The place was rich with history. Sonny was excited. Unbeknownst to anyone else, he felt at peace there. It felt as if a nostalgic awakening enveloped in his mental. A sense of belonging fulfilled him. There were actual alligators passing across the enclosed habitat. Amber noticed the reptiles were acting agitated as they neared. Some scurried out of the water as if being chased by some invisible force. On both sides of the embankment they appeared. They didn't move. All was still. Then it dawned on Amber; the creatures made a clear path for them to pass. Sonny giggled and waved.

"What do you make of that?" asked Amber.

Gertrude answered, "I don't know. I've never witnessed gators act that strange." She gazed at the creatures standing passively. "It's as if they are paying homage to us." Gertrude chortled as they continued onward.

Less eventful, the day moved onward. They returned to the cottage for a good meal and relaxation. Sonny was asleep as soon as his head hit the pillow. His dreams were vivid and animated.

18.

Amber was in a deep sleep. She was awakened by taps on her shoulder. Opening her eyes, she saw Sonny standing near the bed. It took Amber a moment to distinguish reality from the unusual dream she experienced. Worst case scenarios came to mind. She snapped up and out of bed. Taking to her knees, she placed her hands on Sonny's shoulders. She stared directly into his eyes.

"What is it son? Are you okay?"

Looking at his mother, Sonny nodded his head. "Mommy they keep telling me to come with them." His voice sounded dreamy.

She grabbed him tighter. "Who? Who is telling you to come? Come where?" She waited anxiously for a reply. Amber didn't mean to frighten him.

"I don't know Mommy. They're talking to me in my head. There are lots of them. Can you hear them?"

Amber waited a moment as if listening for a sound to emit before responding. "N-no baby, I can't hear them. Tell me what they're saying?"

"Return to the swampland. They said they have been waiting on their leader for eons."

Amber was astonished and didn't know how to respond. "Maybe you were just having a dream babe. Sometimes our dreams can be so vivid we take them for the real thing. That's probably what you did. You mistook it for reality." Sonny didn't respond. "Com' on, I'll make you a hot chocolate and tuck you into bed."

The next morning Gertrude found Amber hovering over a hot, cup of coffee. Amber didn't hear her enter the room. Her mind was preoccupied with thoughts of Sonny. Gertrude cleared her throat in an effort to make her presence known.

"Good morning. I didn't hear you come in." Amber took a sip of her steamy, hot beverage. "Would you like some coffee?"

"Sure," Gertrude took a seat at the table.

Amber stood, she walked over to the island in the middle of the kitchen and poured coffee into a cup. She placed the cup in front of Gertrude.

Gertrude was wearing a lavender colored housecoat. She noticed Amber's hands were slightly trembling. She touched her hand after she placed the cup down and gazed into her eyes. "Sit." Gertrude waited for Amber to return to her seat. "What' going on?"

Amber sighed deeply. She didn't want to say anything, nor become troublesome. It was the sincere concern that Gertrude portrayed that melted away any guard that Amber may have had. "I was awakened by Sonny tapping me on the shoulder. He was scared. He said voices were telling him to return to the swampland. Something about he's their leader."

"He's a child. Maybe he was having a bad dream."

"I thought the same. Gertrude you have been so good to me. I want to explain something to you. I should have told you a long time ago. My father said what raped me wasn't human. That is why he was so against me having my child. My mind is now asking questions."

"Okay, let's get him checked."

"Okay."

19.

Amber and Gertrude sat in the waiting room of her private doctor. Both stood abruptly when a doctor entered the room. Amber was the first to reach him as he entered. To Amber he didn't look like a doctor. He wore an expensive designer suit with equally elegant shoes. He was well-groomed. His smile exposed perfect teeth.

"Is he going to be okay?" asked Amber.

"We've done a series of tests. Some of which will take time to received the results. The test that I do have data for is the psychological test. I did the Rorschach test. His results are normal in that aspect."

Amber studied him strangely. "What is the Rorschach test?" She asked quizzically.

"Herman Rorschach was a Swiss psychiatrist from the 1920's. His development focuses on personality and intelligence using inkblot designs. The designs that reveal intellectual and emotional factors. It's a very effective tool."

"So what's the conclusion?" asked Gertrude anxiously.

"Sonny has done well but I am concerned with the fact he thinks he hears voices. Some children develop these symptoms as a defense mechanism against something troubling in their lives. These fictitious characters can just be a way of coping. Most times when we locate the problem at the source and fix it the characters soon vanish."

"So, are you saying he's having home issues that I am probably not aware of? What can I do about it if I don't' know what they are?"

"I'll address that in a moment. There's another thing that is troubling. His blood shows inconsistent activity. The DNA shows part of the genetic code is of a totally different species. The DNA codes are from a warm-blooded reptile." The doctor scratched his head in bewilderment.

Gertrude listened without interruption. She was intrigued by the explanation from the doctor. She recollected the time they were in the swampland and witnessed how strange the animals were reacting to Sonny's presence. It was beginning to make sense. *'Maybe her father was on to something.'*

"What can be done?" asked Amber. A sense of urgency was in her tone of voice.

"The only thing that can be done at this time is to let things run their course. Keep a close monitor on him. If there are any home issues, please address them. That includes school. You know how mean classmates can be at times." The doctor hesitated as another thought occurred. "I was meaning to ask about the father. Could he be the factor? Maybe there is some unrecognizable agent running through his veins. Maybe his genetic makeup can explain what we're dealing with."

"His father is unknown." She noticed the puzzling expression on the doctor's face. "I was raped. I don't believe in abortions." Amber felt somewhat embarrassed.

"I see." The doctor rubbed his chin as he contemplated the scenario. "I'll notify you when the rest of the test are concluded."

Sonny was in school the very next day. He asked for a bathroom pass. It was customary to give a ten minute pass to the students. Sonny moved about in the quiet hallway as he headed directly to the bathroom. Upon exiting, he gave notice to how much luster the waxed floors reflected and how they glistened from the fluorescent lighting. The hallways were lightly decorated with school memorabilia. A few wood and glass showcases were in the hallway. The showcases is where most of the school's achievements were housed. There were plaques and trophies on display. He noticed a round brass metal, it brought about an ineffable sensation. Sonny didn't understand the sensation. At that moment, a guard wearing a blue uniform with brass buttons approached.

"Shouldn't you be in class? How much time is left on your hall pass?" His baritone voice was stern. Sonny was startled. He adverted his attention from the glass display to the guard. The guard was in his mid 40's. He displayed the beginning of a receding hairline. His nose was puffy and red with a slight outbreak of pimples. His skin contrasted with his jet black hair. His beetle brows scared most of the children. Sonny was confused with the unfamiliar sensation. An indescribable awareness is what he felt. His emotions were that of fury. The perception was foreign. A rage shot emitted from deep within. A force so great, on a molecular level, his body reacted. Sonny's fingernails grew outward at an amazing velocity. They were sharp as razors. A fury of hatred unsheathe from deep within. It was an outcry from his ancestors. Sonny's eyes were fixated on the brass buttons on the uniform. He brought his hand up across the neck of the guard slicing a deep gash into his throat. It happened so quickly the guard didn't have time to react. The cut was so precise, the wound didn't bleed right away. Sonny looked up at the guard emotionless. His demeanor was as if nothing was wrong.

"I have all the time in the world. It is you who doesn't."

Reflexively, the guard's hand covered his throat. It was too late. His thyroid cartilage was severed. Blood gushed forth from his open wound. The gash flowed like an unattended faucet. The guard's life force ebbed from his body. His blood-soaked hands did nothing to prevent his demise. Leakage found its way onto the lustrously, polished floor. The crimson liquid began turning the waxed surface into a rainbow of redness.

Normality returned to Sonny. Finding an awkward joy in the act, Sonny returned to class. Not one fragment of blood splatter touched him. He interacted with his school work as if nothing transpired.

A bell sounded. It was usually the recess bell that caused the commotion, only the time didn't coincide with the sound. The teacher made an urgent announcement. "Children we are going to the auditorium for a town hall meeting. I want everyone to be quiet and move in an orderly fashion." She had been informed by telephone of the tragedy. They were not sure if the perpetrator was still in the building. After the Sandy Hook incident, which drew national attention, no one was taking any chances. *'How could something like this happen? Especially in a school?'* She escorted the last child into the auditorium. She glanced down the corridor at the commotion that prevailed. She left the children with another teacher. She closed the door behind the last child and locked it. She headed down the hall. There were security guards and police officers present. Some uniformed, some were plainclothes detectives, along with emergency medical technicians. They were busy at the scene. A gurney stood upright in the middle of the hall. Men were hovered in the corner near the display showcase. Looking around at all the strangers in the school, she recognized one of the guards. She headed in his direction.

"Jerry what is going on?" Her voice was a whisper.

"Parker was killed. We don't know who did it but we have the building locked down. If the perpetrator is still on the premises we'll find him or them." His voice was agitated.

Parents were called in to pick up their children. Amber and Gertrude were devastated after receiving the news. The school incident frightened them. They prayed that Sonny wasn't hurt. After finding he was safe, they decided to return back to New York. They didn't want anything to tie him into something that could bring attention to his situation. Later that evening, they finished eating a hearty dinner. They were packed and ready to leave in the morning.

"Mommy, can I go play out back for a little while? Please? This is my last day here."

Amber looked toward Gertrude for support. She received a nod of approval. She adverted her attention to Sonny. "Okay, but don't go far. I want you back in the house in 90 minutes. Don't have me go looking for you. Do you understand?"

"Yes, ma'am." Sonny rushed out of the house to play.

"It will be his last day here. It may do him good to wander and reflect. This is good, safe land. You don't have anything to worry about," stated Gertrude.

20.

Officer Wainwright couldn't believed his fortune. He had just hung up the receiver after talking with the Center For Disease Control in Atlanta. The samples sent to them earlier were because of their use of the most sophisticated testing equipment available. He had been notified of another inquiry that matched the exact DNA samples sent to them years ago. The information gave new hope in the search for Amber. Officer Wainwright wasn't angry with his daughter anymore. He just missed her dearly and wanted her back. He understood the pressure she was under. *'I should have been more compassionate.'*

"At least I have a location to start from." He spoke aloud into the empty office. Excited about the information, Officer Wainwright called his wife to give her an update on the situation. He knew that would bring her some relief. Since Amber's disappearance, their relationship had been strained. He let her know that he was on his way to Florida. Although it was out of his jurisdiction he was given permission by the upper brass to find his daughter. They in turn notified the Florida authorities that one of their own was on the way. It was strictly a gesture of courtesy to let Officer Wainwright visit.

Using the free time he was allotted, Sonny secretly obeyed the voices inside his head. Their frequency had been getting stronger. The tones were becoming more demanding. At times he couldn't think of anything else. Sonny headed toward the swampland. He wasn't afraid of walking alone. As he neared deeper into the wetlands, Sonny could hear splashing sounds all around. The agitation in the water was profound. The rattling of leaves began to crescendo all around him. He realized his vision had changed. He was able to inspect his surrounding in an entirely new way. His brain adapted to seeing and deciphering two images simultaneously. Each eye captured a different image to his vision. He noticed the water creatures on the riverbank. They scurried along on both sides of the bank. The river's edge was filled with alligators, lizards, and snakes of different descriptions. There were chameleons, and other small ground crawlers. They all remained still and at attention. Sonny also remained motionless. He was in awe at the communication and recognition that was being displayed. He tried to interpret their intentions. He could feel the energy from all of the species. He was able to decipher the force he felt into a knowing, a natural instinct. Sonny was able to translated the dynamism into a language he could understand. Sonny discovered he was revered as royalty. He was the supreme manifestation of millions of years of evolution. Each genus paid homage for an enlightening future. All communication was done through psyche. Sonny made his way back home. The very next day, Sonny and his family were heading to New York.

***

Officer Wainwright exited the commercial aircraft at the local airport. The courtesy call afforded him a uniformed officer awaiting him in an unmarked sedan. He was escorted to the Florida Keys Police Department. Due to the nature of the visit, they were happy to oblige.

Officer Wainwright was taken directly to the hospital where the inquiry for the DNA had been requested. The follow-up there led him to a cottage. To his dismay the place was abandoned. With the trail running cold, Officer Wainwright headed home. With the name of Gertrude Pemberton to go on, he would do more research.

When he reached Shottenville, a call awaited him. The caller was from Washington, DC. It was the Pentagon. They wanted to do testing on his daughter.

"Good luck," he retorted. "If you find her tell her I'm also looking for her. Tell her I miss her." He hung up the receiver frustrated. *'What the hell is going on?'*

21.

UNITED STATES DEPARTMENT OF DEFENSE
SCIENTIFIC RESEARCH DIVISION
PENTAGON BUILDING/PART B
ARLINGTON, VIRGINIA

Two accredited scientist sat in a conference room on high back, leather seats. They were examining documents on a huge rectangular mahogany wood table. The surface of the table was polished to a glossy sheen. They also viewed an animated description of the latest results of their viral examples on a huge screen. Both men were in their late 50's, each was from a different field of study. Dr Parkerson is an Ivy League professor in the field of genetic research. Dr Collins was well versed in culture grafting.

They had been studying the samples of the mysterious DNA that they received years ago from a victim in Shottenville, Louisiana. It had been forwarded to them by the CDC. Protocol measures were used to assure all agencies were on the same page. After the 911 tragedy in New York, a new measure of security became priority. With the recent samples sent to them from the Florida Keys, they had information that the person of interest was still alive, or the possibilities of others.

"Tom, I think we're dealing with extraterrestrials."

"Be it as it may, I think I've broken the genetic code. I have been able to clone the cultures. To each one I've introduced a different host. I am able to amalgamate the two into becoming one. In the process allowed, both genes remain independent of the other while existing together. Only, there is more testing needed and no human host to test on."

"Are you saying the two cells can coexist and dominate one another depending on the circumstances?" Dr Parker rubbed his chin in deep contemplation.

"That is exactly what I am hypothesizing, only the strain is getting weaker as I try to mass produce. I don't have control over its fusion."

Dr Collins studied the screen. "So you're saying we need the actual host to be more effective?

"Yes." Dr Parker nodded his head profusely. "That's exactly what I am talking about."

"So, where do we find him?"

"Well, this last sample was called in from a doctor at the Florida Keys on an unstable little boy named Sonny Wainwright."

"Okay, we'll request a search team to find him."

22.

Back in New York, Sonny found a new purpose in life. The wilderness that surrounded his house was no longer just a place that added beauty to the area. He discovered his alliances were there. Not fully understanding, he knew his past, present, and future were there.

Sonny awoke feeling energized. He sat on the edge of the bed before stirring. He thought about the puzzling episode in Florida. Although baffled, he was not afraid. Sonny felt powerful. He gazed at his fingers. He studied them as if they were foreign objects. Sonny recalled the transformation. He didn't realize how, why, or what caused the reaction he experienced with the guard. He knew there was a reason for it. An idea occurred. Placing on his clothing, Sonny headed downstairs to eat breakfast.

Afterward, he mounted his bicycle and began heading toward the woods.

There weren't as many exotic animals in Long Island, New York as there were in the Florida Keys. Sonny felt he was in tune and able to connect with every entity that operated on the same frequency. Sonny used an old cypress tree as a backrest to relax as he viewed his surroundings.

Unexpectedly, a slight chill erupted within. His body began going through another metamorphosis. One that was similar to what his father had experienced and his ancestors before him. He was able to exchange his molecular structure with that of the tree. At that moment, Sonny was no longer in the physical characteristics as a human. He was now a part of the tree's trunk. To the human eye he was invisible. Sonny remained still as he heard a noise oncoming. As the noise intensified, it brought along two park rangers. They were adorned in forest-green uniforms. They wore wide brim, felt hats. The hats were the color branch-brown. The earth tone colored uniforms also included brass buttons sewn down the middle of the garments. The men were doing a routine survey on the deer population in the area. It was necessary information for determining the length of open season for the hunters. The men were equipped with binoculars, note pads, holstered weapons, and citation booklets. They approached the tree where Sonny was now interfused.

"I think the population in this area is prime for hunting this season," said a forest rangers. He stopped and sat near the very same tree with Sonny. He looked over and saw an odd object. "I wonder who left this bike here unattended?"

"Com' on, we still have the ravine to check out before it gets late.

Don't forget we have to get a look at the bass in the lake." His partner stood. He dusted off his uniform. The two men headed toward the ravine.

"I am sure they'll be back for it."

***

Gertrude was enjoying a peaceful moment in the garden. She had just finished working on her roses and was delighted with a spiked tea drink. The alcoholic beverage relaxed her. Sitting in her easy chair, with her face poised up toward the sun and feeling the exhilarating warmth upon her face, she opened her eyes to see two men wearing dark colored suits heading toward her from the black, granite walkway. The pathway led to the rear of the house from the roadway. The sounds of birds chirped. The prominent sounds of leaves gently flapping in the wind were audible. Gertrude braced herself for their visit. Their demeanor and stature screamed law enforcement in her mind. *'I hope they're not here for Amber.'*

The two men approached. Simultaneously, they displayed their identification cards and badges. Gertrude inspected them. She noticed the two men held similar features. The thought of them being related came to mind.

"Mrs Pemberton?"

"Yes, what can I do for you?"

"We're sorry to bother you. I'm Agent Tescar." He gestured toward his partner. "This is Agent Taylor. We're sorry to intrude on your privacy but we are following up on a lead. We are looking for a woman. Her name is Amber Wainwright. She went missing about a decade ago. We were told you brought a young boy into a hospital in the Florida Keys. We are hoping the boy is an offspring of that very woman."

"Well, I don't know much of what you are taking about. Besides my bringing in a neighbor's child to the hospital for a routine checkup isn't against the law the last time I checked. Mind you, the mother was along. You see her vehicle was disabled and she had no way of getting there. Is there something wrong about that?"

The two looked toward one another; they adverted their attention back to her. Quickly, one of the agents glanced at the surrounding area nonchalantly. "No, there isn't. We're sorry to bother you." They retreated toward their vehicle.

Inside the quiet confines of the sedan, the agents conversed.

"She's lying."

"I can feel it also. But why is she protecting Amber?"

"I don't know but we'll find out soon enough."

"Remember, she has a lot of clout in Washington, DC. Her husband was friends of advocate lobbyists there. That means we have to tread easy."

23.

Amber and Sonny returned to the house from an after-school project. Upon entering, they noticed Gertrude was in a somber state of mind. They saw her sitting on the sofa in the living room staring into nothingness. Amber approached with concern.

"What is it Gert? Are you not feeling well?" Amber went close and stooped to one knee to Gertrude's eye level.

"Child, some people came here looking for you and Sonny. Initially, I thought it to be your father making an inquiry about you. When they introduced themselves as federal agents, I knew it was much more than an inquiry of your father looking for his daughter. I don't think he has the clout to investigate me. How would he? They asked about Sonny."

"How do they know about him? I have been very cautious about leaving a paper trail."

"I've thought about that also. What I'm getting from it is someone leaked information recently. The only one I can suspect is the doctor. How else would they know where I am?" Gertrude paused to contemplate even more. "My husband had plenty of influence in Washington. What I am going to do is call in a marker and see what comes back." She stood with the help of Amber and headed into the study room.

Sonny and Amber were in the kitchen sitting at the table. The tabletop was littered with books, magazines, and other paraphernalia. They were researching a project for school. Sonny was enthusiastic about it. Suddenly, Gertrude entered.

"I just knew it! It was that damn doctor. Well, when he sent for the test results on the blood sampling, it was protocol that the samples be shared with the FBI forensic department in Washington, DC. Well, it matched something they were researching."

"So, what does that mean?"

"It means they're not going to stop searching until they find him. We must leave here…" Gertrude noticed Amber's nervousness. She touched her shoulders to comfort her. "Don't you worry. Gert is resourceful." She eyed Amber directly. "Your son is different; we know that. I know a place where they will not bother us."

Amber's eyes swelled with tears. Unable to control her emotions, moisture flowed down her rosy cheeks. "I know Sonny is different. My father was right about what he perceived. What do I do?"

"I think it's time for us to speak directly to Sonny. We have to know for sure. Even if it's something out of the ordinary, at least we'll know. It doesn't change the way we feel about him."

Amber adverted her attention to Sonny, who was continuously working on his school lesson. She walked over to him. "Baby, I want you to go to your room for a while. You can play with your video game until we get there."

"Okay."

Amber watched her son march off toward his room. She adverted her attention back to Gertrude. "I guess you're right." They conversed a little more. They were mindful to keep their voices low.

***

After knocking on the door, Amber and Gertrude entered Sonny's bedroom. He was playing a video game with a headset on. Sonny didn't hear them enter, but he felt their presence. A keen sensation alerted him. He turned, taking off his headset.

"Hi Mom, hey Aunt Gert, what's up?" They saw him smile. He was growing into his own person. Sonny didn't favor either of them physically, yet he loved them both. His smile was bright and warming.

Amber sat on a chest near the bed. Gertrude took a seat on the twin-size bed. The room was typically decorated for a teen. There was an area where he kept his music. The walls were plastered with posters of sport figures. "Son, we need to have a word with you. Do you feel up to it?"

Sonny looked at the two women in his life. He felt a vibration sensation along his spinal column as he looked into their eyes. It was as if the sensation were becoming words. At that moment he was able to read their thoughts. "I know what you're here for." He placed the headset on a chair. Taking a seat, he faced the two. "You're here because you want to know what I am. To tell you the truth, I don't know either. I know I am different from most guys. That is why I am always by myself. It's cool because I can make my own decisions." He stared directly at his mother. "I know how I was conceived. It's as if I was there to witness my own birth. See, I come from a long lineage of my kind."

"W-what do you mean?"

"Mom, I'm different. I think you know that. You just didn't know how to tell me. So, I found out on my own. I don't know how to control it yet, but I can blend into live objects. One time my fingers began to change right before my eyes."

Amber and Gertrude were astounded by the explanation. They were both caught off guard. After glancing at one another, they adverted their attention to Sonny.

"Okay, things will be all right son." Amber used the opportunity to explain what she knew, holding nothing back. She explained his conception and how his grandfather felt about it. How his name was attributed to her real soulmate. "You see, your grandfather knew this could happen and was strictly against it. That is why we're here."

Sonny took in all that was said. Everything began making sense. "What now?"

Gertrude interjected. "We leave! I have other properties in the country and abroad we can use."

"When?"

"As soon as we can pack a few things. I'll get our passports and paperwork in order."

24.

Officer Wainwright was in his office going over a domestic abuse complaint. A self-conscious man wearing a charcoal, gray suit, white shirt, and gray tie entered the room. Officer Wainwright gazed at the man with an outstretched hand.

"Officer Wainwright? I'm Agent Adelphi. We spoke earlier on the telephone."

Officer Wainwright stood to received the greeting gesture. "Yes, please have a seat." He glanced at his desktop, then at the agent. "You'll have to excuse the mess. Duty calls." He felt sheepish.

"Please, I understand. You should see my office." He waved it off. "I'm here to share information with you and maybe you can do the same."

"Sure, shoot..."

"Okay, this is what is known at this time. We feel we have a lead on the whereabouts of your daughter." The agent noticed he held the officer's attention. "The trace led us to the Florida Keys. Do you know anyone that lives in that state? Someone she could be living with?"

"Florida?" Officer Wainwright shook his head. "We have no family in Florida."

The agent believed him because of his quick response. His training helped in the observation. "The person she's with name is Gertrude Pemberton. She's a wealthy widow. She has places all over the country and abroad. There were tests done on your grandson, I think they referred to him as Sonny."

"Sonny? What test?" Officer Wainwright was now bewildered.

"Why? Is there something you want to add?" The agent looked on skeptically.

"Sonny was my daughter's deceased boyfriend's name. He died trying to save her."

"Sonny was brought to a doctor in the Florida Keys for some psychiatric test and blood work. That's when the red flags came into view. He came across our radar because whenever any test are done with blood, it must go through a database that flags and profiles for any possible criminal activities. Sonny was an exact to DNA match we received years ago from you. We went to follow up and she's gone. We are now checking other locations."

"Please, if there is anything I can do from my end let me know."

"Will do." The agent stood. The two men shook hands. Officer Wainwright escorted him out of the building.

***

Agent Adelphi sat in the field office talking on the telephone. He was ecstatic after receiving approval for a trace on Gertrude Pemberton. Her accounts and properties were now at his disposal to view. After disconnecting the line, he turned on his computer and began accessing information. *'Okay, what are you up to Mrs Pemberton?'* He began doing his research on the data accessed.

***

Gertrude Pemberton had received a call on her cellphone. She was informed of the inquiry into her assets by the government. Her lawyer forewarned her to make the necessary adjustments before the window closed from a federal stoppages on all her accounts. She explained to him what was needed. The call was disconnected. "I'll dare them fools probe me; I've done nothing wrong." She looked to Amber and Sonny. "Come on, we're getting out of here. We don't need anything. We'll get what we need when we get where we are going."

25.

JOHN F. KENNEDY INTERNATIONAL AIRPORT
DEPARTURE SECTION/ C
8:20 PM

Gertrude Pemberton, along with Amber and Sonny, exited a taxicab in front of the departure building. There were commuters standing around. Some were using skycap service to get taxi services and luggage services. The area was busy and moving. Gertrude knew the arrangements of the airport service all too well. She and her late husband had been all over the globe through the friendly skies. She knew it would be busy at that time of the evening. She used the commuter congestion to plan their exit away from the scrutinizing eyes of the authorities. Every moment was timed to get them safely aboard Flight 702 to Switzerland. From there, they would move onto Venezuela. They rushed into the building through the electronic, self-opening doors. The glass partition parted as they neared.

The group was dressed in plain, dark clothing. They blended in with other commuters. In effort to not draw attention, Gertrude made arrangements through a third party to secure the tickets needed to board the plane. Without carrying luggage, they were able to bypass certain check points. They headed toward the departure ramp. Gertrude spotted a man standing near the entrance. He was dressed in a plain, black suit. She noticed his shoes didn't match his outfit. They were black, combat boots. Gertrude prided herself on attentiveness to detail. He was talking on a cellphone. Mindfully keeping their heads down as they walked, the group continued forward. Gertrude was relieved when they passed the man in question. She glanced at her wristwatch noticing they were early. *'At least we're here.'* As soon as they cleared the entrance to the ramp, two men converged on the scene. The men were dressed in uniforms. They wore dark blue suits with lustrous brass buttons. They were airport security employees.

"Excuse me ladies. Can you please follow us?" Each guard held a grip on the arms of the two ladies while their other hands were near their unfastened, holstered sidearms. They were trying to be as discreet as possible to avoid a scene in the busy terminal.

"Follow you to where? What is the meaning of this? We have a plane to catch," retorted Gertrude. She was obviously irritated at the interruption.

"We have a few questions."

"There's no time. We have a plane to catch." She looked at her wristwatch. "We have…"

The officer interjected. "I'm sorry ma'am, you'll have to come with us."

"For what?" Her voice rose to anger. Passersby looked on at the commotion. Gertrude saw some using their cellphones cameras to record the event.

"That will be told to you." The officer's grasps tightened. "Please don't make a scene."

During the confrontation of words, no one paid any attention to Sonny. He stood observing the entire scene from a personal perspective. Deep inside of his body a change was taking place. His eyes were focused on the brass buttons on the officer's uniforms. He didn't understand why he was attracted to them, but for a strange reason they caused an internal fire to ignite inside his being. Slowly, his body's chemistry and molecular compounds began a metamorphosis.

"Well, if it's me you want let the others go."

"Sorry, everyone is being detained for questioning at this time. Please come with us."

Feeling helpless, Gertrude submitted to the request of the authorities. The three were escorted through the corridor toward a stainless-steel door. As they approached, Gertrude continued to glance at the boarding ramp to freedom as it slowly ebbed out of her reach.

They entered through a steel door. A long hallway came into view. The corridor was barren of people. White, tile floors made up the decor of the setting. The wall were concrete painted gray. Further down the corridor more doors existed. Each one held a large glass observation window. On the inside of the room the glass was mirrored. It reflected a one-way view from the inside. As they neared, something anomalously happened. The event was almost cynical and diabolical in retrospect.

Sonny held onto Amber's hand as his began to transform. His little fingers and nails began to grow elongated. His eyes began to take on a shape resembling that of a reptile. Sonny's skin became scaly with a reptilian-like texture. His height took on another dimension. With everyone in complete bewilderment and awe, the officers began reaching for their weapons. In a quick fluid motion, Sonny reacted with the speed of light. His razor sharp nails found their way against the throat of one of the adversaries. Blood spewed out of its open wound. Reflectively, all the officer could do was hold his throat with both hands. From pure apprehension, the other officer struggled to unholster his weapon. That was the extent of his defensive action. Razor-like nails belonging to Sonny moved across his wrist like a surgical scalpel. The officer's hand was severed from the wrist. The act was done with so much force and speed, the removal of his extremity was unimaginably swift. The officer didn't feel any pain at first. It wasn't until he viewed what happened. That's when shock signals were sent to the brain and the pain registered. Blood gushed from his open wound with so much force all the officer could do was stand still, unmoving and silent. He was in a state of shock. His body fell to the ground from the loss of blood.

Amber was amazed and stunned. She stood motionless, not knowing what to feel or do. Mentally, she questioned Sonny as to being her own offspring. Her father's words resonated in her head. The scene was gruesome. Amber remained motionless and in total disbelief. Gertrude seized the moment as she watched Sonny return to normal. He stood still as if not knowing what had transpired. Gertrude took Amber by the hands tugging her out of the door with Sonny in tow.

They headed out of the door mixing with the busy flow of commuters. The sounds of footsteps, luggage being handled, and with people chatting, resonated in the area. Their hearts raced as they headed toward Gate 12. The plane was just about ready for departure.

Just making it in time to board, they entered the aircraft finding their seats in the first-class section. They sat while breathing laboriously. Nervousness was on display. Everyone remained quiet trying to process what had taken place. The incident seemed surreal, an unbelievable story if told. The passenger door closed. The no smoking light illuminated. Instructions about the flight were given to the passengers via the public address system. The plane taxied the runway and was finally in flight. Gertrude knew it wasn't over. She was aware they could be apprehended at the next stop. Her mind worked frantically for a solution.

26.

Sonny was sound asleep in a seat next to Amber and Gertrude. The first-class section was only semi-filled with commuters. The nocturnal setting outside obscured visual view of the celestial.

In effort to relax, Amber listened to music on her headset. Gertrude stared straight ahead. She was envisioning the incident that transpired. The episode was hard for her to wrap her mind around. She glanced over at Amber. Their eyes locked on one another. Amber removed her headset. She kept her voice low to a whisper.

"I'm scared Gertrude. I don't know what to do next. You saw what happened back there. My father was right. He foretold this; he knew this would happen. He only wanted to spare me grief."

"Okay, so what? Did you see why Sonny did it? He did it for us, to save us. No matter what, we know he loves us. He'll never turn on us."

"Not yet! Who's to say it won't happen? What if one day he will not be able to control his powers?"

"Well, it hasn't happen. Right now we need to focus on getting to our destination. There will be people there that can get us into Venezuela. From that point onward we will be untouchable from the United States because Venezuela don't have an expedition agreement with the states. They're considered foes."

The sound of an announcer suddenly blared in the quarters. The sudden, sharp tone captured everyone's attention.

"Ladies and gentlemen you are directed to return to your seat and apply your safety belts. We are making an emergency landing at the nearest airport to eject a sick passenger. We are sorry for the inconvenience." The sound emitted from hidden speakers in the ceiling.

Amber was startled. "W-what do you think that was about?"

"I think they found those officers," stated Gertrude.

"What now?"

"I don't know child!" exclaimed Gertrude. She became agitated. "Let me think…"

***

Officer Wainwright received information on the whereabout of Amber and her son. He was also informed about the situation. "Please don't hurt them. I'll be right there." He replaced the receiver on the cradle and began packing a few items into a suitcase. Afterward, he headed out of the door.

Using this personal vehicle, Officer Wainwright headed toward the airport. As frustration mounted, he slammed his hand on the steering wheel. "I knew this could happen," he shouted in the confine space.

***

Amber gazed at her son as he slept. The feeling of hopelessness had subsided. She wasn't afraid anymore. She knew what needed to be done. She tapped Gertrude's shoulder to gain her attention. Amber spoke low and confident.

"Gert, you've done wonders for us. I can't risk getting you anymore involved than you are already. We love you. You've helped me enough. I never would have made it this far without you. You're definitely a godsend. When we land, I want you to tell them your actions were forced by the creature. They'll check the tapes and see Sonny's transformation. They'll believe you. Now, we have to go."

"Where are you going? What will you do?"

"Don't you worry, the less you know the better. They'll release you because it's us they're searching for."

"Okay here…" She retrieved an ink pen from her pocket. "Give me your arm. Hurry, there's not much time left." She began writing a series of numbers on Amber's inner right forearm.

Amber studied the numbers curiously. "What is this?"

"It's cash. Those are numbers to an account. When you get where you need to be, just access it from anywhere. Spend whatever you need. I'll never spend it all in my life time. I'm too old child." Tears swelled in each one's eyes. They embraced empathetically, feeling one another's pain.

"Please, let Sonny sleep until I get back." Amber stood. She gestured with a wink toward Gertrude as she headed toward the rear of the aircraft. Amber reached the restroom. As she was about to enter, a stewardess approached.

"Miss you have to return to your seat."

"Please, I have to take my insulin. Can you please help me? My sugar level is rising. It will only take a moment."

The stewardess eyed the young woman in distress. She herself remembered having to inject her own mother when she was home. She made her decision. "Okay." Both women entered the restroom area. The door was closed behind them.

A few moments after, Amber exited the restroom alone. She was now adorned in an airline stewardess uniform. Using the key she removed from the stewardess' pocket, she locked the restroom door. Amber headed toward the first-class section from which she came.

***

Gertrude's mind was preoccupied in thought when Amber returned dressed as a flight stewardess. "I'm not going to ask." She watched as Amber gently shook Sonny to awake him.

Moments later, they headed toward the rear of the plane. She didn't turn around. If she had, she would have collapsed from the emotional strain of having to leave her best friend and second mother behind. Amber realized she was fortunate to have met Gertrude. Not many people will have the opportunity to experience the love and nurture Gertrude provided.

27.

THOMAS BURDEN INTERNATIONAL AIRPORT
BURNSVILLE, MINNESOTA
RUNWAY 6 NORTH/GATE 12
9:33 PM

The 727 Boeing jetliner came to a full stop in front of Terminal C. On the tarmac, emergency and law enforcement vehicles were parked strategically. The formation blocked the aircraft's path. Lights flashed atop the vehicles displaying a kaleidoscope of colors around the perimeter.

Armed officers, along with plainclothes, federal agents surrounded the aircraft. Their weapons were drawn. An order was soon given, the men breached the aircraft.

Law enforcement personnel forcefully entered the cabin. They yelled commands. Startled passengers obeyed the orders. The commotion inside of the fuselage was intense. The passengers were astonished and fearful. Confusion controlled the moment. Using the element of surprise as an advantage, the agents and officers thrusted forward and throughout the fuselage. Each passenger was led through a screening and checked for identification. When it was Gertrude's turn, she had no worries because she had access to the best lawyers in the country. *'They'll make it look like I littered on the sidewalk.'* She was apprehended. Gertrude went along quietly. Her mind was on Amber and Sonny. *'Please, let them get through this ordeal.'*

After the passenger's manifest was checked off and the staff was accounted for, they noticed three of the members were missing from the roster. One staff and two passengers.

"Search down below in the cargo area," ordered the lead agent. The men dispersed throughout the aircraft looking for a woman and child.

***

Amber walked away from the scene more fearful for the welfare of her son. *'No matter who or what, I gave birth to him. I'm his mother.'* She only left him behind at the request of Sonny. Her mind recollected the moments.

"It's okay Mom. You go ahead and I'll go below. I'll be okay. I will meet you at the nearest diner in town. At midnight we'll meet again. Don't worry. I can blend in with things. They'll never suspect anything different." He gave her a reassuring wink of his eye.

***

Agents were assigned to check below the aircraft. They came across oversize luggage, boxes, and animal cages. The sound of dogs barking and cats purring resonated. The drone of the engine inside the pressurized cabin was profound. Agents inspected the entire area looking for the two missing passengers. Nothing turned up. They were surprised to see the carcass of a cat. The lifeless body was contorted, but not bloodied.

"That is very strange," said one of the agents from the federal bureau. They continued to search. The men were recalled to the upper deck.

"I want all surveillance camera footage of the perps. I want captions of them entering the buildings and boarding the aircraft," ordered the high ranking official of the investigation. "I will interrogate the woman myself."

***

As the evening arrived, the commotion of the day subsided. The entire airport was under seizure for inspection. National Guards stood watch over the aircraft until the investigation was completed.

Below, in the cargo area, a cage was opened. A hellbender crawled out of the confined space. It made its way toward the landing gear's wheel well enclosure. It continued down the shaft of the mechanism heading onto the tarmac. The hellbender continued its trek onto the runway. Although it was night, the reptile's eyes illuminated from the energy radiated by the moonlight.

The incredible physical aspect of the salamander was its size and dimension. Six inches in length, it was amazing that so many internal organs and bio-systems could fit into its tiny frame. The colors of the outer shell was astounding. A chromatic spectrum radiating from its exterior. Most creatures of its kind were harmless. This particular one was deadly. It traveled on the black tarmac toward the perimeter's fencing. The nightcrawler used the nocturnal setting as a cover.

Suddenly, a raccoon appeared from the darkness. It blocked the path of the salamander. Both creatures had illuminated eyes. The raccoon spotted the usual easy prey as it headed toward the perimeter, a place it could not enter because of its size. Food was all the raccoon sought. The hellbender salamander would normally be no match for the huge raccoon. Without forewarning, a pink tongue was exposed. The organ was three times the length of the reptile's body. The tongue exited the mouth of the hellbender at an alarming rate of speed. Carrying on the tip of the tongue was a highly toxic resin. The substance was instantly absorbed into the skin upon contact. The tongue of the lizard connection with the leg of the raccoon proved fatal. The raccoon reflexively hopped back, only it was too late. The deadly venom was quickly absorbed into the bloodstream. The raccoon lie powerless in a state of paralysis. Within seconds the highly potent potassium bromide concentrate caused the raccoon's heart to stop functioning. It died painlessly. The salamander continued onward through the perimeter fencing. Suddenly, the hellbender salamander began going through another transmutation. Its body began to contort into what looked like a painful stature. The salamander's body began to stretch and grow in length and diameter. Its molecular composition changed drastically. The hydrogen, carbon, and nitrogen ratio distribution caused the matter to change entities. Before long, Sonny materialized out of the mass of matter. He was naked. Although his mind was clouded, he could remember certain things of the past. The most pronounce remembrance of his cognizance was of his mother. Deep inside his mental he was aware he had to be someplace to meet her.

Continuing on his journey, Sonny's mind was preoccupied in thoughts. He didn't feel the bushes a they pricked his naked body. Sonny knew he had to find clothing fast. In the far distance, the sound of a dog barking resonated. Sonny headed in that direction. Minutes later, a house came into view. Sonny exited the wooded area and approached the house from the rear. He spotted clothing hanging on a clothesline by wooden clothespins. The dog was aware of his presence and continue to bark. Sonny made his way toward the clothesline. Finding pants and a tee shirt, he quickly swiped them. He found a pair of shoes on the porch. With the items in hand, he quickly headed into the wooded area from whence he came.

Adorning ill-fitting clothing, Sonny headed toward the destination to find his mother. His surroundings were unfamiliar. He felt her energy within. He looked up toward the sky at a bright star. Using the astral, he navigated to where he knew she would be located.

28.

Amber sat in a diner nursing a cup of coffee and a cheese danish. She was tempted to purchase another setting for Sonny. She knew he would appear. There was no doubt in her belief. The diner was quiet at that hour except for a few truckers conversing. There were three waitresses on duty attending to the customers. Their black uniforms with white lace trim were dainty. The delightful aroma of bacon, eggs, and coffee moved through the air. Amber checked her watch. It was 11:55 am. She took a sip of her warm beverage and gestured for a waitress.

A middle-aged woman sauntered over. "Yes, what can I get you?" She wore excessive makeup; her lips were painted crimson. The waitress chewed gum as she talked. Her writing pad was positioned at the ready to take an order.

"A breakfast delight and a coffee please," said Amber. After the waitress left to retrieved the order, she checked her wristwatch again. It was now midnight. A strange feeling overcame her. Her heart felt like the bottom had fallen out.

The food arrived shortly after. Amber picked up the menu to busy herself. An unexpected hand touched her shoulder. Without looking around, she smiled. It was a knowing.

"I knew you'd come. Here…." She gestured with her hand to a seat across from her. "Have a seat son. Eat while your breakfast is still warm."

Sonny took a seat. He glanced at his mother, then to the food in front of him. The aroma of the food delighted his senses. Being near her warmed him emotionally. It gave him a sense of security. Without words he began to eat. He didn't realize how famished he truly was. Sonny began devouring his food at an alarming rate. Particles of food were on the side of his lips as he chewed feverishly.

Amber felt terrible to see him so disarrayed and hungry. She wanted to question him how he escaped unnoticed, but she thought better. *'The focus is getting away safely.'* She noticed the food on his plate was finished. "Would you like more?"

Sonny denied the offer by shaking his head. He picked up a glass of orange juice and began gulping it down. Finished, he wiped his mouth with the back of his hand. "Mom, I see the way you look at me. I sense you are afraid. Don't deny it. If the shoe were on the other foot I would be afraid also. Please, know that I love you mama. I know I am different. Maybe I can use it to protect us."

Amber studied his eyes. She felt a heartwarming sensation along with a sense of security. "Son, I think that it's time to go home. It's time you met your grandparents."

29.

Officer Wainwright sat in his office. His desk was cluttered with files and backlogged documents. His mind drifted in and out of work. The recent information about Amber and his grandson sparked a new energy within. His relationship with his wife was troubled because of the ordeal. The news had given them hope. Now, with the trail running cold again, there was nothing more he could do. A dark emotional cloud had resurfaced. He sat and gazed out of the window. Officer Wainwright didn't hear the knocks on the door, nor when Sergeant Carter entered the room.

"Ughm...." The feigned sound of throat clearing was audible. It was done to make his presence known. "John?"

Officer Wainwright slowly adjusted his vision from the outdoors to the room. "Hey Ron, what's up? What can I do for you?"

"No! What can I do for you?"

"What do you mean?"

"I'm not trying to pry. I know it's been hard on you and the Mrs. I am worried about you that's all. Your attention hasn't been on your work lately. That can be a bad thing given what we do for a living."

"What do you suppose I do?" His voice rose an octave. "Sit at home and worry myself to death? Have you any idea of what I'm going through? My daughter ran away to have a baby by god-knows-what." Emotions overcame him. Using his hands, he shielded his face. He tried to mask the tears that forced their way through his eye ducts.

"John…" Sergeant Carter placed a hand on Officer Wainwright's shoulder. "You are not alone. We are with you. Anything you need done we're here for you."

"Thank you."

"Why don't you go home? We can take it from here. If things change we'll call you. I'm sure the Mrs could use the company."

"Maybe you're right."

***

Officer Wainwright entered his ranch-styled home. His wife was out shopping. Sometimes he dreaded going home. With Amber gone the ambiance wasn't the same. He and his wife hardly displayed affection. Their relationship was strained.

Officer Wainwright flopped on the plush, leather couch. The brown colored couch and the cream colored rug were a lovely color scheme in the living room. He used the remote device to turn on the television. Officer Wainwright always tuned in on the news. Subconsciously, he'd hoped to hear news about Amber. Standing, he headed to the wet bar at the corner of the room. He poured himself a scotch, whiskey, and water. His movement stopped suddenly as his eyes were transfixed on the mantle near the bar. His focus was on framed pictures of his family during happier times. Amber was 12 years old in one of the photographs. She was holding her first-place soccer trophy. He remembered the time as if it were yesterday. *'Where has all the time gone?'* He sighed deeply.

Returning to the couch with his drink in hand, Officer Wainwright's attention was on the news. A vehicle was hit by a freight train at a railroad crossing. Suddenly, a knock came to the door. *'Meredith must have forgotten her keys again.'* Officer Wainwright placed his glass down and stood. He headed toward the front door. He opened the door as amazement overwhelmed him. His mind took a moment to processed what he was witnessing. He couldn't believe it. Trying to find his voice was not effortless. Officer Wainwright was suffering from a mild mental paralysis. Tears of endearment flowed from his eye ducts. He looked downward at a handsome, little boy. He recognized the eyes. They were the same color as Amber's. His attention went to his daughter. He was surprised at her facial change. He noticed the hardened features. Being a father he recognized the look. It was the appearance of life in the fast lane. The world had aged her quickly. She was still beautiful. He hadn't seen her for more than a decade. The two eyes locked. Both were experiencing mixed emotions. Feelings of hurt, anger, empathy, and forgiveness was on both their minds. Mr Wainwright opened the door wider. This was the day he'd prayed for ever since her abrupt disappearance. He knew he would never make that mistake again. The domino effect had caused his family much grief.

"Please, come in honey. I am glad you're home. Wait until your mother gets back."

Amber wasted no time, she hugged her father at the threshold. The emotional release of pent up emotions caused the floodgates to reopen. Pride had caused her so much grief. "Daddy, I've never stopped loving you." The embrace was heartfelt by both.

"Get in here."

Inside the house, Mr Wainwright took to one knee. He was now eye level with Sonny. "What's your name? Do you know who I am?" He studied the boy who was his grandson.

Sonny nodded. "You are my grandpa."

"You bet I am. Are you hungry?"

Sonny looked to his mother who gave her approval. Sonny nodded his head eagerly. "Yes."

"Okay, come with me. We'll find something tasty for you." He adverted his attention to his daughter. "Your room is just the way you left it." Mr Wainwright escorted Sonny into the kitchen.

"Have a seat." He gestured to a white marble top island. Sonny sat on a wooden stool with a soft, white, leather seat. He remained quiet and observant to his newly discovered surroundings and grandfather.

Mr Wainwright headed toward the refrigerator. Opening it, he peered in at the shelves filled with many different foods. Although it was just two of them living in the house, stocking the shelves had been a ritual since Amber was a young child. "Okay, let's see." He adverted his attention to Sonny while standing with the refrigerator door open. "What would you like? Breakfast? Lunch? Dinner? Anything you want you will get, and if it's not in here I will go and get it. How does that sound?"

Sonny smiled. He liked his grandfather immediately. "Anything you are having grandpa is okay with me."

"Okay." Mr Wainwright began retrieving food items from the refrigerator. He placed them on the counter. Meticulously, he began preparing a dish from all the ingredients he selected. "So tell me, do you like sports?"

Sonny shrugged his shoulders. "I don't know. I've never played before."

Mr Wainwright stopped his preparation of the food. He was astounded by the response from Sonny. "No? Why is that?"

He looked away embarrassed. "No one has ever taught me."

"Okay, we'll just have to fix that." Mr Wainwright adverted his attention to the preparation of the food. The delightful aroma drifted through the air. It was the mixed scent of Spanish omelets, bacon, cheese, toast, and freshly squeezed orange juice. When the food was done, he set out two placemats and placed the steaming plates of food. Grace was said before anyone ate. Sonny bowed his head out of respect. He didn't know what else to do. Although his mother was a spiritual person, she wasn't very religious. With what she'd endured over the years, she didn't have the time to teach Sonny the ins and outs of the popular dogmas.

The two ate in silence for a while. Each one savored the delightful taste of the foods. Mr Wainwright noticed Sonny was famished.

"Sonny, I wanted to say I admire your honesty. There's an old adage that says, 'to know that you don't know is best. To pretend to know when you do not is a disease'. They continued eating.

***

Amber climbed to the top of the white, wooden staircase with alabaster carving on the handcrafted banister. The balusters caught her attention because she remembered scratching numbers into each one with a pen knife. Being there caused the floodgate of recollections to soar out of control. She remembered growing up in that house feeling safe and secure. At the top of the stairs a narrow, green carpeted corridor came into view. Family pictures hung along both sides of the walls. Amber stopped to gaze at the photographs. A warm feeling enveloped her. Two doors over was her room. Gently, she turned the brass doorknob on the white door. She opened it slowly. The reason for the unhurried motion was mostly because she wanted to savor that moment.

The room came into view. Just as her father said, everything was the way she'd remembered from more than a decade ago. Amber stood in the middle of the room admiring her surroundings. She couldn't believe she had made the decision to leave it all behind to entertain an unknown fate. Gertrude crossed her mind. She looked at her forearm and remembered the numbers that Gertrude placed there. Walking toward her study desk, she rewrote the numbers on a slip of paper and placed it into her pocket. The next thing she did was flop upon her queen-size bed. Mixed emotions resurfaced as she stared up at the ceiling. Happy years of her childhood returned to the forefront of her thoughts. Suddenly, the sadness of that warm, summer night in the cornfield crept in her mental view. It seemed like just yesterday to her. The thought from the aftermath from that terrible ordeal resurfaced. The unknown creature that took Sonny from her was still traumatizing.

A knock came to the door.

Slowly it opened. Her father's head peered in. "Do you mind if I come in?"

"Sure, come in."

He entered slowly, using the time to formulate the words he wanted to carefully convey. "How do you feel honey?"

"Honestly? Afraid and unsure. Dad, I know what I did was wrong and I should have considered what you were saying."

Her father interjected by raising his hand as a gesture. He knew how emotionally painful the conversation was. "You don't have to say anything honey. Whatever it is we'll work it out together."

"No, I want to say it. I have to get things out of my system before I burst. It was a bad time for me. I was scared and confused. I will say this to you; the ordeal has broadened my horizons about life and that little boy downstairs. Yes, it's as you said. He's an anomaly. But, he's still the most loving and caring person I ever wanted to know. I do not for a second have any regrets for having him."

He took a seat in a chair next to the bed where Amber sat upright. "What do you mean by anomaly?"

Amber spoke in a low tone. "He's different, just as you said. At first I was frightened beyond anything imaginable, but I know he loves me and will protect me."

"So, what does anomaly mean?"

"It means that he can change into living things. Somehow, the animals in the wildlife recognized his significance and were subservient to him. You see…." She explained the past decade of her life to her father. He sat quiet and occasionally nodding as he absorbed the bizarre story.

"Babe, I have to be honest with you. It sounds like a sci-fi novel." He snapped his fingers as a thought occurred. His facial expression turned serious. "Honey with everything you're telling me, it's not safe to stay here. Men from the defense department have been here inquiring about you and Sonny. That's how I knew I had a grandson. If what you say is also known by them, it maybe the reason they want to get their hands on Sonny. Probably for tests of some kind. We cannot let that happen. Come on, we're going to the next state. We can find a place where they won't expect to find you. Now, tell me about this lady that helped you over the years."

Amber explained to him about Gertrude. "Dad, she was an angel in disguise. Can you please make sure she's okay?"

"Yes, I will see what can be done. Right now you should eat. Come down when you are ready. Sonny is in the guest bed sound asleep. I guess he's had enough for one day."

"Okay, I'll wash up and join you downstairs."

As Amber and her father ate, the sounds of keys being inserted into the lock resonated. The mechanical sound of the lock mechanism being turned resounded in the room. Amber stopped chewing. She knew who was at the door. Anxiety overwhelmed her. The door opened with her mother entering with grocery bags clutched in her arms. Amber's father had his back to the door as he sat at the table. He turned his head in effort to get a first-hand glance at his wife's surprised facial expression.

The unexpected happened. The groceries fell from her grasp. She collapsed on the floor unmoving. The two bolted from their seats to her aid. Mr Wainwright did CPR while Amber held her hand. "Call 911!" Amber hurried off.

She returned quickly. "They said they'll get here in five minutes."

"Amber you have to go upstairs. Stay out of sight. I don't want anyone to know you're here. We don't know if the defense department is outside lurking about. I think it was the over excitement that captivated her."

"All right Daddy."

30.

The evening after the ordeal with Mrs Wainwright, the house was back to serenity. Sonny slept through the entire calamity. Mrs Wainwright remained in bed after returning home from the hospital. Her diagnosis revealed she experienced an anxiety attack. The intensity of it caused her body to go into shock. She was given Valium, a tranquilizer used to relax the patient. Mrs Wainwright was in a deep sleep.

Amber and her father looked in on her and headed downstairs to talk. They entered into the den. Mr Wainwright headed to the wet bar and poured himself a drink.

"Would you like one?"

"I'll just have a ginger ale with lemon." They sat on a comfortable sofa next to one another. "Dad, I'm going to move on."

"I know. Tomorrow we're going to the next town."

"No, I think I should just go alone. I don't want to cause you any grief. I just got here and look what happened to Mom."

"Don't think that way. We love you. Why is that so hard to understand?"

"I know you love me. I've learned in life a person has to explore things on their own to gain experience. I know it's only a mistake if I don't learn from my encounters, and it's just a lesson if I do. You taught me that."

Mr Wainwright realized his little girl had matured. "So, where will you go? What will you live on? You said yourself Gertrude is out of the picture."

"Not quite." She sighed deeply. "She'd extended her generosity so I would be looked after." Amber noticed her father held a facial expression of bewilderment and disappointment "Don't worry, I'll be okay. As soon as I get wherever it his I'm going, I will notify you." She stood and he followed suit. The two embraced compassionately. "Dad we'll be leaving in the morning."

"What about your mother? It will kill her to know you were here and departed again without a trace. How can you do that to her?"

"You said so yourself agents from the Department of Defense were inquiring about us. How do you know we aren't being observed at this moment, or that the house isn't bugged?"

Mr Wainwright was silent. "If your mother doesn't awake in time, I will make her understand. Now, you go and get some rest."

"Okay Daddy." After checking in on Sonny, Amber returned to her bedroom to lie down. She was sound asleep within minutes.

***

Mr Wainwright's mind formulated different scenarios to end the drama that his daughter was experiencing. He'd truly wanted it to end so his family could resume their lives. *'It's the boy they want. It's him that's causing all the commotion in the first place.'* His thoughts became vivid. He raised out of bed quietly and headed for the guest room. Reaching the door, he stood for a moment staring at it. His mind constantly conjured thoughts justifying what he would do. He rotated the brass doorknob slowly. The hinges squeaked slightly at the pressure of being turned. The door opened inward to a darkened room. As he opened the door wider, the dimly lit hallway invaded the darkness. It illuminated a silhouette in the room. Mr Wainwright's vision adjusted to the darkness. He saw the mound under the cover. Sonny was in bed resting peacefully. Mr Wainwright stood over Sonny watching him sleep. His heart rate soared. *'If he's no more there wouldn't be anymore problems.'* He thought. *'How can I think like this?'* He heard a noise from behind. His attention focused toward the sound.

"What is it Dad?" Amber's voice was a whisper. She stood behind her father.

"Nothing." He turned to face her. "I was just admiring my grandson. Everything is so new."

Amber grasped his hand. Quietly, she led him out of the room. Gently, she closed the door behind. "Come on Dad, I want to have a talk with you." They headed downstairs toward the study.

Amber sat next to her father on the sofa. She angled her position enabling her to gaze directly in her father's eyes. "Daddy, I am scared.

I don't know what I've gotten myself into. Sonny is a loving boy, but I've seen something inside of him that isn't worldly. He's never tried to hurt me in any way. He only protected me. Inside my twisted thoughts I questioned what if things changed. I should have listened to you."

Her father placed a finger to her lips, the gesture was to discontinue her sentence. "Don't say that." Her words fortified the guilt he felt previously when he visited Sonny. "We have a situation we'll deal with together. I must admit, I had strong dislikes for the situation. In the end I love you. Whatever the consequences are, we'll deal with them as a family. That is the most important thing to me."

ONE

WEEK

PRIOR

31.

Agent Proctor worked for the Department of Defense for eight years. He graduated from the Massachusetts Institute of Technology ahead of his class. His major was digital design. He was a bright computer analyst and an energetic man in his late 20's. The Department of Defense sent him to gather information. His assignment was to access the owner of the blood samples. The samples they discovered years prior was still a mystery to them. They realized capturing the host would have endless possibilities.

The agent arrived at Officer Wainwright's home knowing the officer wouldn't be present. He went to the rear of the house and cut power wires in the junction box. He raced up the pole that held the communication panel for the entire block. Proctor was dressed as a local cable man. His uniform included a blue jacket, jeans, and a utility belt filled with tools. A patch phone dangled from his tool belt. He waited. One hour later his phone rang.

"Shottenville power company. May I help you?" His voice was masked to a deeper tone than normal. He listened to the response of the caller. "Yes, there's a unit in the area as we speak. He will be there within minutes. His name is Curtis Branch." Agent Proctor disconnected the line. A smile formed from his thoughts. *'This is child's play.'* Descending the utility pole, he headed toward the house. He knocked on the door. It was quickly opened by a woman wearing a green, polyester suit.

Mrs Wainwright looked at the uniformed gentleman standing at the threshold. She noticed he wore a helmet and a utility belt. "They said a few minutes but I never believed it."

"Yes, my name is Curtis Branch." He displayed his fraudulent identification. "I'll have to come in and check the power lines." He looked at the house next door. "I don't think it's a major problem because the others on the block seem to have power. It won't take long." Agent Proctor went from room to room. He looked to see if the person in question was there. Inside his tool box were wireless cameras, listening devices, and voice activated recording equipment. Within minutes he was finished.

"Mrs Wainwright, I think I found the culprit. Your power should be restored momentarily." He exited the house and headed directly around back to restore the connection he initially disconnected.

Inside the cargo section of the step van, monitors, voice recognition equipment, and other digital equipment were mounted. Agent Proctor moved the vehicle to a safe distance from the residence. He began monitoring Officer Wainwright's home from the rear of the truck.

32.

Three men sat around a rectangular table in a conference room. The location was the United States Department of Defense building. It was a closed meeting, only authorized personnel were attendance. The subject of discussion was Project Chameleon.

"Okay gentlemen, we're making progress. Even though the existing cultures are strained beyond us making more intense discoveries, fear not. We have intelligence that has located the source of this strain." A discordant hum hovered in the room. The speaker's name was Director Charles. He was a heavyset man with a pudgy, oval face. Early signs of turkey chin was evident, the loose skin drooped under the chin. His voice was deep baritone. He wore an ash-gray suit, black tie, and a lighter shade gray, button-up shirt. The roar of chatter subsided.

The head of the genetic scientists on board began to speak. His voice held a southern twang. He spoke properly. "I think this new strain along with the knowledge we have will surely give way to a new frontier of defense."

Walter Broden was a neuroscientist. He was an elderly man with thick lens eyewear. His features displayed a stubby nose and double chin. "If we can link the neuron cells to the brain, we'll have created a trigger that will allow us to project energy at will."

"Okay gentlemen, I will keep you posted on the events as they unfold. Remember, as soon as we have the principal specimen in our custody, I want you here and ready for work. Time could be of the essence in this case." The meeting was over. Everyone stood and began exiting the conference room.

***

A small team of federal agents were dressed in combat gear. They wore blue, windbreaker jackets with bright-yellow letters on the back that read FEDERAL AGENT. They were at the ready position. Their caps held the Department of Defense acronyms. Their demeanors displayed no nonsense. The men exited a tactical truck with a predetermined destination. There was no room for compromise.

The team separated into four different groups. They surrounded the house on the quiet cul-de-sac. One hundred feet up the road was a black step van. It was the mobile tactical command post. Inside was equipped with monitors, computer equipment, communication, and visual consoles. Three men monitored the station.

The four teams waited in position. Soon after, an order was given. The teams surrounded the sides and rear of the house. The group in front was ordered to enter. Using stealth movements, they approached the house. Each man wore a helmet with goggles. Their weapons were drawn. The teams were given direct orders from the command center.

Using a battering ram, the front door was compromised. As it fell off the hinges, the men rushed into the house. Using their tactical training and their advanced knowledge of the layout, they began advancing throughout the house. They entered different rooms simultaneously.

The house was quiet. Everyone inside was in their designated resting places. Suddenly, deafening explosion of sound erupted in the room. Bright light and smoke filled the space. Flash bang explosives were used to disorient the occupants inside the residence. None of the occupants were prepared for the invasion. Everyone was astounded and disoriented. Mr Wainwright bolted upward from his bed. His first thought was a dream. He reached for the weapon he kept on the night stand. The 9mm, semi-automatic, handgun was holstered. The time it took for him to unfasten and handle the weapon proved to be fatal. A single muffled sound was followed by a hot, white flash. The weapon ejected a deadly projectile into his cranium at point-blank range. Officer Wainwright was only able to see the yellow insignia on the cap of his assailant. Afterward, his world became silent, dark, and void of sensation.

Mrs Wainwright was in her bed. She was still under a medically induced sleep from the prescription drug administered to her by her physician. Never was she aware of what was taking place, nor did she feel her life force ebbing from her body. Her life being extinguished was unknown or felt. Only the dreams she was having suddenly did not exist anymore. It was like watching a movie and the reel on a projector suddenly ran out of film. Instead of the white illuminated screen associated with it, for Mrs Wainwright, there was only blackness, silence, and no sensation. The agent stood directly over her after aiming his weapon and placing a single projectile into her heart.

Amber heard the commotion. She jumped out of bed to see what the disturbance was all about. She went to the window to see what appeared to be government men around the house. Witnessing that gave her a slight sense of fear. Hurrying to the bedroom door she saw uniformed men rushing into the house. From her vantage point upstairs, she only thought of Sonny. She knew why there were there. Barefooted, Amber rushed toward his room. She was intercepted by a masked, uniformed soldier. He shouted incomprehensible orders but Amber didn't comprehend its meaning. Her focus was on getting to Sonny.

Suddenly, she felt a sharp, hot, and searing pain in the back of her neck. A bright light flashed intensively then a loud noise followed. A rancid scent of blood and guts associated with the assassinations permeated the air. Then the sights and sounds happened again. This time it was only for an instance. A heightened pain penetrated again. Then all things ceased to exist for Amber.

The agent continued onward in search for others. After the onslaught was fulfilled, two other agents joined him. It was there when something unusual happened. Putting away their weapons, they retrieved their special sidearms. Sonny was quickly awakened by the disturbance. His senses were heightened. A knowing existed. He knew he was under attack. His body chemistry anticipated by changing its molecular structure ratio, causing his entire body to begin changing form. The process was slow and needed to be completed before he could defend himself. His fingers and fingernails became elongated. His nails were razor sharp.

The bedroom door burst open. Sonny tried to react, but was too slow because of his undeveloped anatomy. The agents pointed their weapons at him. One of them fired, hitting him in the leg. Moments after, Sonny felt his energy being drained from his body at an alarming rate. The last image imbedded in his mind was the floor racing toward his face.

***

Inside the command center the men were ecstatic over the news. There was a loud cheer from the guys that monitored the electronic equipment.

"Okay, I want our eyewitnesses on the scene." He looked over to the communication analyst. "Call it in."

***

After the tactical personnel were gone, the local authorities were on the scene. There were spectators, emergency vehicles, and local news reporters gathered about the area. It quickly became chaotic. The place was cordoned off with police tape to keep the crime scene from being contaminated. Police, local, and state authorities began gathering on the scene and sharing information.

One witness was asked what happened. "I was driving by and I saw a van loaded with guys jumping out and running into that house. I knew it wasn't official business because the guys wore bandanas around their faces. They wore dark clothing; a few had gang writing on their backs. I couldn't make out what it read because it was too dark. I slowed for a moment, then took off and called you guys." The federal eyewitness did exactly what he was paid to do.

THE

DISCOVERY

32.

THE UNITED STATES DEPARTMENT OF DEFENSE RESEARCH CENTER/ C
GENETIC MOLECULAR RESEARCH AREA
7:20 AM

A series of people adorned in white, laboratory coats, goggles, latex gloves, and shoe protectors were moving about the sterile environment. The walls were made of stainless steel, the same material made up the work stations. Glass cabinets held an assortment of medications and other type of chemicals. The employees adorned face masks with shields to fend off the possibility of contamination.

Located in an isolation chamber, Sonny was in a medically induced coma. He was also restrained. There were intravenous tubes running from his arm to machines. Clear fluid entered him from another machine. In addition, a machine next to the bed emitted soft, tapping sounds. More tubes ran from that machine into Sonny's leg. Those tubes were filled with a crimson color liquid. The machine was extracting his blood. It slowly returned it after the blood had been filtered and analyzed. The scientist needed all the data they could obtain in the event the host died.

Sonny lie on a gurney dressed in a white gown. He seemed to be in a peaceful sleep. He had no clue of the events that transpired previously.

During the next couple of months, test were performed with his blood. Tissue samples were taken. The researchers became worried that keeping Sonny in a dormant state could effect his physical and molecular structure. They decided to revive him to see if they could witness and analyze the traits he possessed. They would then make adaptations. The researchers used simulated examples of an enormous snake and a frog. When the frog was struck and poisoned by the deadly viper, instead of being paralyzed as any other prey would have been, the frog used the venom in a new enchanting way for survival. The once harmless frog now possessed a poisonous substance in its blood and on its tongue. If eaten, it would definitely kill the host. The same research went into using Sonny and the other creatures. It was a long drawn-out trial and error process.

Sonny's eyes opened to a bright light. The illumination was from an overhead fluorescent lighting fixture. His eyes shifted in its orbs in efforts to distinguish his whereabouts. His mind raced as he tried to recall the past. His cognizance was blurred. Images of his mother appeared mentally. Trying to move, he felt aches and pain in his joints. He noticed his movements were restricted. Tilting his head, Sonny became aware his limbs were shackled to the bed railings. He began to panic. He didn't know his whereabouts, nor why he was placed in that predicament. He wasn't aware of the hidden cameras throughout the area. Researchers worked around the clock monitoring Sonny.

Sonny placed his head on the pillow and looked up at the ceiling. His thoughts were scattered about his ancestral past. Images of his mother, Gertrude, and his grandfather came into his mental perception. Suddenly, his captors entered his mental space. Something strange began to take place inside of Sonny's body. His mind could feel it. A pressurized warmth began building in his core. He could feel his internal organs changing with his outer extremities. Instantly, he felt the urge to gag. He tilted his head forward so he could see the shackles on his feet and hands. Without warning, a pink organ ejected from his mouth. It was a moist, fleshy substance. It stopped stretching as it made contact with his leg shackle. It moved to the other. Instead of retracting, it reached his two wrist shackles. Upon contact, the tongue left a potent residue on the steel restraints. The residue held a powerful acidic substance. The chemical agent began to penetrate the steel. It withered the steel to a soft gel. The action resulted in the shackle's dismantle. Fragments of metal fell to the floor.

Sonny was now free. He realized there was much to his physical capabilities that surprised him. He jumped out of bed. There was pain in his leg and arm joints from a lack of mobility. He rubbed at his limbs to improve circulation. Wearing only his gown, he ran to the huge, glass mirror. He knew he was being observed. Sonny banged on the glass.

"Did you see that? Can you believe this?" stated a technician in the observation room.

"It just keeps on getting better."

"Wait until we show this to the director." There were two observers in the booth at the time. They were taking notes and recording the activities in the closed confinement area.

"I think you're right." A yellow dial was turned.

***

A large cloud of steam erupted from the sprinkler system. It caused the room to be filled with a thick, white cloud. A substance in the steam was mixed with a vaporized tranquilizer called chlorpromazine. Within minutes, Sonny was brought under control. His body collapsed on the tile floor. Attendants dressed in white uniforms rushed into the confined space. Sonny's unconscious body was placed onto the bed. More test were done; more research was enacted from the ordeal. The researchers realized they were witnessing the tip of the iceberg.

FIFTEEN

YEARS

LATER

34.

Much time expired when the director from the Department of Defense figured that Sonny would test well if he were allowed to go into the wild to perform. It was decided the agency couldn't afford to let him loose in public for safety reasons. To rectify the situation, they decided to build a full scale county for him to roam. Every detail from an actual county would be included. They made sure nothing would be left out. Every inch of county would be under their scrutiny.

The model was erected and placed in a desolate area in Louisiana. Every detail mattered to achieve perfection. The county was fenced in by an impregnable border. There were no view or interference from the outside. They created man-made swamplands. All the creatures associated with that geography were included in the area. No detail was overlooked. The researchers noticed Sonny's cells matured to a certain level and remained in a dormant stage thereafter.

A huge monitoring station was built adjacent to the enormous compound. More than 200 researchers were employed around the clock to monitor Sonny's movements. Even as he slept and washed.

Sonny was released into the swampland after undergoing a psychological evaluation and indoctrination that erased part of his memory. They didn't want him to dwell on the fate of his family. He was still under a calmative prescription. He was programmed with the thoughts of having recently escaped his captors and reached a town called Carlsdale, Louisiana. In reality, the location was 130 miles from the Capitol.

***

Sonny returned to consciousness from a drug induced slumber. He was fully dressed, and carried a wallet filled with cash. His joints were stiff and sore from immobility. Sonny stretched deeply. His mind was clouded with mirky thoughts. He awoke feeling famished. His eyes moved around inspecting his unfamiliar surroundings. He wondered how he arrived there. His attention was on a thick and tall Cyprus trees. He noticed the landscaping and the wildlife associated with the forest. Birds chirped, deers romped, leaves flapped in the cool, mild breeze. He noticed the sun was positioned directly above. Using that measure, he estimated the current time to be about midday.

Sonny shook the tiredness away. He proceeded on foot toward a clearing to the south of him. Three quarter mile ahead, a town loomed into focus. Its scale began to grow in size the more he neared.

Sonny exited the clearing feeling as if he leaped from one time zone into another. Sights and sound suddenly became pronounced. He was astounded. He gazed around to see automobiles moving about on a roadway. There were shops on both sides of the street. The area was the town's main street. People walked on both sides of the sidewalk. Some were shopping. There were people standing around conversing on the sidewalk. Sonny took in the scene. His thoughts were still clouded. His senses picked up a delightful aroma. The scent of pizza, pepperoni, and garlic waft through the air. He followed the smell.

A quaint, nostalgic pizzeria came into focus. Sonny entered. Bells on the door jingled as he opened the door. There were booth seating. He headed toward the counter. No patrons were in attendance. Tending the counter was a man in his mid 40's. He wore a apron around his waist.

"Good day, what can I get you?" asked the clerk. Sonny was suddenly dumbfounded. He'd never thought about having cash to pay for anything. Everything felt strange to him. He placed his hand in his pocket. To his surprise, he retrieved a wad of cash. He studied the money for a moment. He was baffled as to where it came from.

"Is everything okay son?"

Sonny was returned from his reverie to the attention of the clerk.

"Uh? Two pepperoni slices and a large ice tea."

"Okay, you go find you a seat. I'll have a fresh pie coming out of the oven in a moment. It'll be nice and hot just for you."

Sonny sat enjoying his food while looking out the window at the movement on the streets. Nothing made sense to him. His thoughts were scrambled. He couldn't remember his past. He felt as if he appeared from nowhere. *'Where do I come from? How did I get here? What is this place?'* His thoughts were puzzling. He glanced around the shop. He noticed it was unoccupied. The clerk was busy preparing another pie. "Excuse me sir." Sonny gained the clerk's attention. "Where is this place located?"

The clerk studied the young man. His expression displayed bewilderment. "We are at 879 Main Street."

"No! I don't mean street address. I mean what state is this?"

The clerk acted as if he was taken aback with the question. "You're in Saint Francis Parish, Blackstone, Louisiana. Is everything all right?"

"Yes, I just wanted to make sure." Sonny was no longer hungry. He paid his bill, then exited the pizzeria.

The warmth of the sun felt good on his skin. Sonny needed a place to rest in order to get his thoughts in order. He walked down Main Street until he came to a side street. He headed down that block. On the left side of the street a sign hung from a pole. It read 'Apartment For Rent'. It was an Old Georgian-styled home with white, French shutters attached to the windows. The pitched roof was covered with cranberry colored slate tiles. Walking up three steps led to a porch. Suspended from chains was a cozy swing. It was made from wicker straw. It was painted white. A matching table held a pitcher with glasses. Sonny rang the doorbell. The chime was pleasant to the ears. Moments after, an elderly lady opened the door. The door hinges squealed for oil. The woman stood behind a screen door. She looked at Sonny, then opened the screen door.

"Yes, may I help you?"

Sonny was now able to get a good look at the woman. Her hair was short cropped and silver. Her face displayed age lines. She was wearing a green, summer dress with a beige, paisley design. "I am inquiring about the apartment advertised. Is it still available?"

"It sure is." Her left jaw was protruded from chewing snuff, a powdered form of tobacco. "It's a one bedroom with a walk-in closet, living room, private bathroom with tub and shower. The good thing is that it's furnished. The rent is 300 dollars a month. If you've got the cash you can move in now."

"Can I see it?"

"You sure can." She stepped aside to allow Sonny access. "My name is Miss Gainer but you can call me Mavis."

"My name is Sonny." For a moment Sonny forgot his sir name. "Carter." He received her outstretched hand.

The room was pleasant and comfortable. Sonny flopped onto the king-size bed. Within moments he was fast asleep. He was fully dressed.

35.

Sonny awakened abruptly. He was soaked in perspiration. His mind was disoriented. Suddenly, vivid images flashed across his mind. Faces of people he had no idea who they were appeared mentally. A strange inkling subsisted. He felt he knew them or at least should. The sensation inside of him was great with curiosity. Rising out of bed he headed toward the bathroom to wash up.

After splashing cool water on his face, Sonny adverted his attention to the mirror directly in front of him over the sink. He studied his image. The reflection in front of him was unfamiliar. Oddly, he touched his face hoping to gain recognition. Nothing made sense to him. *'Who am I? How did I get here?'* He checked his rear pants pocket. Retrieving a wallet, he quickly handled it. He opened it. Sonny was surprised to see his picture on a driver's license. Searching the contents, he discovered credit cards with the name Sonny Carter. An idea struck. He hurriedly dressed and exited the apartment.

***

Sonny walked into the town's local bank. A teller was busy with receipts. She noticed Sonny approaching.

"Hi, may I help you?" Her smile was pleasant.

Sonny read her name tag. He noticed she was very pretty with a nice smile. Her eyes were hazel. Her auburn colored hair was done in a French braid hairstyle. "Yes, I would like a statement for my account."

"No problem sir, only you will have to go to the banking official over there." She gestured with her finger. "I can only do transactions from this station."

Her smile warmed him. "Okay, Andrea Banks. Can I ask you another question?"

"Sure, but how do you know my name?" Sonny smiled. He tapped his breast pocket to indicate her name tag. The teller in turn smiled knowingly. "Okay, you got me there. I sometimes forget I am wearing it." Her smile continued to radiate a warming sensation in Sonny.

"I'm glad because your name goes with your face and smile. Your last name goes along with your lifestyle." She giggled amusingly and blushed. "Okay, I will see you again." Sonny headed off to another department in the bank.

Exiting the bank with his statement history didn't tell him as much as he'd hoped. He learned he had a substantial amount of cash in the bank. He was still confused about his lineage. A loneliness engulfed him. Sonny walked down the streets aimlessly. Suddenly, he began to hear faint sounds that were unclear. Initially, they were discordant tones, sounds that slowly became audible voices. None he ever heard. As Sonny walked, he looked around to see if others could hear what he heard. No one paid attention to him as they passed. The voices became commanding in nature. Sonny stopped. He concentrated on the message. After convincing himself he needed to obey the voices, Sonny began walking in the direction in question.

Three quarter mile off of the main roadway, Sonny found himself in the deep forestry. Sonny felt as if he belonged there. The setting was tranquil for him. He sat by a rambling brook. The stream was moving effortlessly. Sonny cast a stone into the water. The rock skimmed the surface a few times before sinking to the bottom. Another strange inkling was felt. Sonny looked around to see wildlife animals had surrounded him. At first he was afraid. The emotion subsided to a calming sensation when he realized the animals were not aggressive toward him. An alligator weighing at least 800 pounds and approximately 15 feet in length came near. Sonny eyed the creature. He wasn't fearful. The creature showed its teeth. Normally, sharp, jagged edges were frightening to the sight. It only eased Sonny. His attention was heightened to everything around him. His vision also became acute. His audible sensation peaked. He felt a strange vibration in his mind that translated into words. At that moment, a communication portal was opened with every wildlife in the forest.

Sonny transmitted first. *'I am confused as to what is happening but I feel that I am amongst my species. What is this place?'*

The alligator transmitted a response on the same frequency. *"You are correct. You are among your own. You come from a long lineage of the reptilian species. You have evolved to the higher consciousness. You are the master of the ages. We are here to serve you."*

"That still doesn't explain how I got here."

"We were gathered from different areas and brought to this place. To our understanding, nothing here is natural. Even the soil is not in its original composition. Throughout the ages our bodies were able to adapt to the different surroundings for survival purposes. The water is somehow treated with an unknown element. You were placed here by other humans. They went away. When you awoke you headed into the town where you abode. You are special, you have the power to change. Use it to your advantage. Remember this place isn't our natural setting. You must get away from here. The humans are constantly watching your every movement. You must redeem us to our highest point." There were no verbal tones being emitted, only vibrational impulses. Sonny heard the homage paid to him by the other species. Soon, they all went about their affairs of survival in the man-made wildlife.

Inside the observatory, the technicians were monitoring Sonny's movement in the artificial environment. His heart rate, blood pressure, and other key vitals were constantly scanned.

"Hey Chuck," exclaimed a technician. "Did you see the way Sonny sat there? All of a sudden other wildlife flocked to him."

"Yes, what has me confused is the aggressive species didn't try to harm him," stated another technician. They continued watching the playback of the encounter on the monitor.

Another technician approached. "Look!" He handed them documented reports of Sonny's vital statistics. "Notice how his vitals heightened as he sat there? His heart rate is off the chart. How can he still be alive with numbers like these?" The others observed the charts also.

"One would think they were communicating on some kind of frequency. I was monitoring his vitals and brain wave impulses and there were no significant changes."

"We'll keep our eyes open and continue to log in everything, no matter how minute it may seem."

36.

Sonny awoke feeling a need to mingle with people. By mid morning, Sonny found himself shopping in a market. The store was busy with patrons. People were milling about purchasing groceries. He pushed his cart onto the frozen food aisle. Selecting a package, he read the ingredients on the back. He continued moving forward with his cart in front of him. Without noticing, Sonny accidentally bumped into another patron that was shopping in the same aisle.

His attention was quickly adverted. "Please forgive me." The woman turned around quickly. To Sonny's surprise his eyes opened wide in pure amazement. "Andrea? Ms Banks? I am so sorry."

Andrea was dressed casually. She wore blue jeans and a tan, cotton sweater with argyle design. Her auburn hair was styled in a French braid twist. Her rosy cheeks and creamy skin complexion was radiant.

Sonny noticed her body was curvy, something that wasn't noticeable from her position at the teller booth in the bank. "That's okay." Curiously, she looked at the package Sonny held. "What are you holding?" Sonny held it up sheepishly for her to inspect. He felt a hint of embarrassment because of the encounter. "That stuff will kill you," she smirked. "When was the last time you had a home cooked meal?"

"Honest? I cannot remember."

"I'll tell you what, I live on Park Terrace near the river. I am inviting you over for dinner and I won't take no for an answer." Andrea handed him a business card with her address and telephone number. "Seven o'clock will be perfect." Andrea continued down the aisle.

Sonny glanced at the card and placed it in his pocket. Excitedly, he finished his shopping. Afterwards, he found a barber shop in the neighborhood. He visited a haberdashery to purchase a few outfits and accessories.

Loaded down with packages, Sonny finally made his way to his room. It was quiet, clean, and cozy. His mind was now on Andrea. He continued playing back their encounter. Sonny had to admit to himself he was attracted to her from the first day he'd saw her at the bank. Now, she was all he could think about. He gazed at his new wristwatch and began to prepare himself for the evening ahead.

A taxicab stopped adjacent to a tall condominium-styled building. Sonny paid the driver and exited the vehicle. He entered the building. Inside, a clerk dressed in uniform stood behind a desk.

"Yes, may I help you sir?"

"Yes, I am here to see Miss Banks. She's expecting me."

"One moment please." The desk clerk picked up the house telephone and dialed. He spoke softly. He adverted his attention to the gentleman standing in front of him. He noticed the young man was handsomely dressed. He wore slacks, loafer shoes, a designer shirt, and a cotton sweater. The color scheme was earth tones. "Who shall I say is calling, Sir?"

"Mr Carter."

"Sure." He continued his conversation on the telephone. He placed the receiver back on the cradle. "You may go up Sir. The elevators are that way." He gestured with his finger. "She is on the seventh floor, door three."

"Thank you." Sonny headed toward the elevator bank. He was nervous. It was his first time with a woman that he could remember. Sonny found the door in question. Just as he was about to knock the front door swung open. His hand was still in the knock position. Andrea stood there dressed casually in a sundress the color of burnt-orange. The hue of the outfit contrasted beautifully with her natural hair color. Her smile was warm and welcoming.

"I'm glad you made it." She glanced at her wristwatch. "And on time, come in." Sonny entered the apartment. "Please sit."

Sonny sat admiring the decor. "This is a nice place you have here. Do you live alone?"

"If course, why do you ask?"

"Oh, no particular reason. This place is quite spacious for a single person. You should see my place. It's nothing like this." He shifted his head to take in the view.

Andrea giggled. "Well, if you saw how much work I do at the bank you would know I deserve these luxuries. Would you like something to drink before dinner?"

"No, I'd rather eat." They headed into the dining room. The area was well decorated and spacious. The table was already set with placemats. Candles were placed in silver, candle holders. The table was festive. A delightful aroma drifted through the house.

The food was set out by Andrea. Everything looked inviting. They began to eat. Sonny felt naturally comfortable in her presence. Seemingly, they didn't have to make small talk. Conversing with one another was genuine.

Sonny dabbed the corner of his lips with a napkin. "I must say this was the tastiest meal I've eaten since I can remember. You're an excellent cook."

"Thank you." She noticed a sudden mood change. Sonny's facial expression displayed sullenness. "What's wrong?" Her tone was that of genuine concern.

"Nothing, I gave my past some thought and please don't think anything weird of me but I can't remember my past."

"Do you mean like yesterday? Last night? A lot of people experience short term memory lost."

Sonny interjected. "No, I mean like my entire beginning."

Andrea was quiet for a moment. "Have you been ill lately? Were you in an accident? It could be anything. How was it you came to the bank when you did?"

Sonny stood. "Can we go into the living room?"

"Sure."

The living room was designed in a modern decor. Chrome and tinted glass were throughout the room. Sonny sat on a plush, brown sofa. Cream colored trim was stitched along the edge of the sofa. The entire set was made with the use of New Zealand lambskin. The texture was soft to the touch. Andrea brought in two glasses of wine. She handed one to Sonny.

"All I can remember was awakening in a wooded area totally disoriented. I didn't even know who I was. I checked my pockets and found a wallet. There were credit cards, identification documents, and other items. The pictures had my resemblance. I went to the bank to get answers to some of my questions. I know now my name is Sonny Carter. I just rented an apartment. You're the first person I've actually met. You've also been so trusting and kind." He smiled. "I hope I'm not freaking you out."

Andrea stared at him for moment. Although she was looking at Sonny, her mind was processing what was revealed. She knew what she was dealing with. Still, she developed a soft spot for Sonny. She liked his honesty. "Maybe it's nothing. A lot of people experience short-term, memory gaps. It could be from overworking conditions. I wouldn't worry about it too much. Would you like to take a stroll on the boulevard? It'll help settle the food we consumed." She giggled.

Sonny really liked her. "Yes, I would love to."

The evening atmosphere was comfortable and pleasant. The temperature was in the mid 70's. The sky was dark and cloudless. The moon was full in the nocturnal sky. Sonny and Andrea walked along the main street conversing. They told one another lighthearted stories. Shops were open. Traffic in both directions on the wide street were filled with automobiles. Walking a little further, they came upon a bar. Inside, a local band was playing music. They entered.

The place was filled with people. The sound of the band filled the room. People sat drinking and listening. Others were on the huge dance floor. They took a booth-seat and ordered non-alcoholic beverages.

"So, what do you think of this?" Andrea had to talk loud over the din in the room.

"I think this is so cool. The band is really good. Do you come here often?"

"I've been here a few times. It's a good relaxer at times."

"Sure."

"You are such a nice person and you are obviously beautiful. Why is it that you don't have a boyfriend?"

Andrea placed her glass on the table. "My job is demanding. Then, it's the problem with the kind of guys I seem to attract. They all seem to be jerks."

"Okay, I understand that. I hope I don't fit into that descriptive category."

"It's your turn. You tell me something about you. What do you do for a living? Obviously, you have a hefty bank account and you are so young. Why aren't you taken? You're an attractive and outgoing guy."

"To be honest with you, I don't know." The question bothered Sonny. It made him feel inept about the situation. "Look, I'm tired. It's been a long day. I had a wonderful time. Can I take you home?"

Andrea looked at him with concern. "Sure, is everything all right? I hope I didn't say anything to offend you."

"No, no, I'm just exhausted. I had a wonderful evening with you and I am looking forward to doing it again."

37.

The observation center was at full swing. A massive number of staff were assigned to the project. Serious thought went into the logistics of building the full-scale project. Data came in, but not as expected. It was a slow learning process. The project was every bit of promising, only the useful information was being revealed sluggardly. There were cameras stationed throughout the facility along with personnel monitoring them. The staff duties were to log information into journals. The operation was huge and costly. The staff worked together throughout the operation. Nothing was left to chance. Every situation introduced to Sonny was rehearsed. Debriefing followed.

Andrea Banks exited the observation center after being debriefed about her encounter with Sonny. Although she gave her statements to the best of her ability, she didn't reveal her true emotional state with the subject. A part of her developed a fondness for Sonny. She began to feel discomfort with the fact that she was unaware of the entire situation. She headed to her quarters to rest and appear at the bank when the time allotted.

***

Sonny slept fitfully in his apartment. He tried desperately to put the pictures of his past to light. He began to have another series of vivid dreams. Perspiration covered his body. His orbs rippled under his closed eyelids. They moved about involuntarily as rapid eye movement continued. His breathing was labored as he viewed the distinctive images of his slumberous state. Visions of people appeared and disappeared sporadically. Although he didn't recognize the images, he felt he should. Images of his mother, Gertrude, his great grandparents, and their parents flashed across his mental vision. The episode was strange. The dream was so vivid, his heart rate rose. His blood pressure heightened along with the reaction. Suddenly, a kaleidoscope of events passed across his mental screen. Unfamiliar to the events, he witnessed the slave traders in attack mode. The Indian campgrounds being pummeled. Many others through his lineage came into view, images he knew nothing about. Sonny took it all in. Realization became evident of who he truly was. He awakened abruptly, he was totally disoriented and drenched in perspiration. He realized he was where he should be. The revelations of his friends in the forest were revealed to him. He understood he must find a way from there. Nothing was what it appeared to be. He dressed and headed out the door.

Daylight was rising. The sky was brilliant with a chromatic spectrum of colors. The iridescence was amazing. Deep purple, red, and yellow painted the celestials. The temperature was cool and brisk. Sonny headed toward the forest. His stride was meaningful with purpose.

***

"What do you think Sonny is up to?" asked an observation technician to a colleague. They were studying the graphic signals of Sonny's vitals as they watched him move about.

"He seems to be in a hurry."

"Let's observe."

***

Sonny stopped at an area adjacent to a creek. Once again, the animals flocked around him. They began their vibrational communication. Sonny was informed of the changes he would experienced, a change that usually happened after decades of evolvement. Because of his controlled setting, his body chemistry was misaligned. He regarded everyone for the information. On his way home, things were now clear to him.

***

Andrea realized her feeling compromised the entire project. She exited her quarters with a frequency scrambler in her pocket. The digital device was a small object that resembled a wristwatch battery. The electronic device was preferred as an operative tool to ward off unwanted frequency receptions during communications. Andrea felt she needed it in order to fulfill her conscientious quest. She dressed and headed for her assigned location.

***

Sonny felt a need to talk with Andrea. He wanted to include her in his plans to depart. He wondered if she knew anything about what was going on. Heading into the bank, he felt a strange inkling. It was an eerie sensation permeating his being. He sensed he was being observed. Heading toward the counter, he saw Andrea staring at him wide-eyed and cheerful.

"Hey," she greeted. She was in the act of counting cash when he approached. "What brings you here? I didn't expect you to be here."

"Well, I really came to tell you that yesterday was special to me." He leaned closer so that he wouldn't be overheard. He whispered. "Is there some place we can talk in private?" Andrea glanced around. She viewed her wristwatch. "At noon, we'll meet at the park." Andrea knew there would only be video and the audio would be muffled.

"Okay, thank you."

The afternoon sun beamed delightful rays upon the forest. The animal life was prosperous. Oak, redwood, and birch trees were plentiful. Sonny and Andrea sat at a stream with their bare feet dangling in and out of the water. The cool water temperature helped to balance out the natural heat that built from him being next to Andrea. She purchased sandwiches along with drinks from the local deli. The two ate while they conversed.

"Thank you for meeting me." Sonny took a sip of his beverage.

Andrea dabbed the corner of her lips. "Don't mention it. Since we are truthful with one another, I want you to know I wanted to speak with you also. But, you go first."

"Okay." Sonny placed the half-eaten sandwich down. "Andrea, before I go further, I want you to know that I like you and I want to be honest with you. There is something going on. I do not know what it is exactly, but I am aiming to find out. Do you have any idea about what I am saying?" Sonny looked directly into Andrea's hazel colored eyes. They reminded him of play marbles. They were called Cat's Eyes. Andrea nervously looked around at her surroundings, she adverted her attention toward Sonny. She withdrew the small electronic device from her pocket. Switching it on, she placed it between them.

"What is-"

Andrea placed her index finger to her lips as a gesturing. "Shhh..." She interjected. Her voice became a whisper. "You are correct with your assumptions. This place isn't what it seems. I know about you being..." She became lost for words to describe Sonny. She hesitated to find the correct word. "Different. You are constantly being observed. I understand what you feel for me because I feel the same for you. It's not what I expected. It feels as if I have to be with you. It's like magnetism is at work here. I must withdraw because this can be considered a conflict of interest. It will only get worst for us."

"Thank you for sharing that. I knew that."

"But how?"

Sonny smiled. He used his hand as a wand, gesturing for Andrea's attention. "They were how I knew."

Startled, Andrea was totally caught off guard at the wildlife that had quietly surrounded them. "Oh my!"

"Don't worry you are safe. I can communicate with them."

Andrea adverted her attention to Sonny. "I'm leaving this place and you have to find a way out also. It is said that you can shape change. If that is true, there is a place near the intersection that can get you out of here."

"Okay, let me ask you something." He looked upward. "Is the sky I'm seeing real? I mean they don't control the skies, am I right?"

Perplexed, Andrea studied him. She looked up. "Well no, how can they? No one can control the skies."

"Okay, how will we meet again?"

"Remember this email." On a slip of paper she wrote her email address. She handed it to Sonny.

Sonny received the paper, placing it into his pocket. "Okay."

Andrea looked around nervously. "I have to be getting back to the bank. They will be looking to debrief me after seeing this encounter. You be careful." She reached for the electronic device that was placed between them. Discretely, she tossed it into the water. Standing, she began walking away. She didn't look back. She didn't want Sonny to see her tear-soaked face. Andrea knew things would never be the same again for her. She felt as if she were acting out a prophecy of sort.

The wildlife animals dispersed. Sonny returned to the apartment. He needed time to figure things out. He felt everything was moving as it should. Although he didn't know the exact details for his life, he was aware he must continue on his path for survival for all those before and after him.

38.

Nothing was the same for Sonny. He ventured out the next day observing his surroundings in a new light. Nothing made sense to him. Throughout the night, he strained his mind to remember the past. It was still a blur. Walking the streets, Sonny felt he was being watched. It reminded him of a laboratory mouse in a giant maze. He sensed he was not being followed, only observed. Sonny needed to find a sanctuary where he could think of a way out. Faint sounds erupted in his mental space. The noise became discordant, then it slowly became coherent. A voice emerged from the contrast of disharmony. Sonny headed toward the forest. It was his favorite place in the artificial land mass. It was there that the natural ability of the other species were able to continue their existence. It reminded Sonny of an adage, *a zebra doesn't lose its stripes just because you've taken it from the wild.* Walking and thinking, Sonny looked up and found himself in the forest. He sat under a tree and closed his eyes. He began feeling a sense of peace. It was an assurance that he wasn't alone, that his plight was associated with others like him. The thought made him ask how many more were like him in existence? He knew he must continue onward at any cost. Sonny allowed the voice to take center stage in his mind. The voice seemed to be omni-present. Its tone and tenor were meaningful. Sonny listened attentively. The words were commanding but delivered with a sense of respect and security. There were instructions conveyed to Sonny. He opened his eyes after the communication ended. He held a sense of knowing afterward. Again, he strongly sensed he was being observed. At that point it didn't matter, his mind was made. Sonny stood. He moved away from the stream. He stood near a full-blossomed, white pine tree. Suddenly, he could feel his body going through an involuntary biological and chemical transformation. He relaxed and allowed it to be. The change was painless. As the ratios of his molecular structure began to change, so did his outer appearance. Sonny's DNA was exactly that of the white pine tree. The transformation was far-fetched. The two shared the same molecular components, only the ratios were different. With the new elements added, his physical features began to be one with the tree. He was now part of the tree. He was invisible to the naked eye.

***

"What the hell is going on here?" exclaimed the observation

technician excitedly. He'd never witness anything as uncanny as this. "Did you see that?" He looked over to his partner for a moment, then continued to watch the screen and the graphic images of Sonny's vitals.

"Yes and no," said another technician. They were adorned in white, laboratory coats. Their name tags were worn on the lapels. "I saw it but I don't believe it. He just disappeared into thin air."

"Look at the digital readings. Some are off the charts, and some are normal."

"Which ones are which?"

"All the vital signs are normal but the body chemistry levels have gone haywire."

"Yes, the reading shows that he is still in existence at that location. I just don't understand it."

"I think we better call this in."

***

To Sonny there were no feelings of change. He felt secure in his new physical appearance. It was a different phenomenon to him. He was able to sense what other plant life experienced. The powerful sun rays gave him strength. The plan was now in motion.

Suddenly, another transformation happened. A pine cone fell from the tree. It rolled next to a rock. The pine cone began to shimmer as it went into a molecular reconstruction. The color changed to rust infused with brown and becoming the color of bronze. The forming of a salamander began to take shape. Sonny didn't fight the feeling. He just allowed what he was experiencing to be. Looking through the eyes of the salamander was clear, only his visual equilibrium was affected. Things that was once small were now humongous. He preferred the bird's eye view of the world. Everything now seemed threatening to his survival. He scurried from the rock undetected. Without warning, an American bald eagle hovered over him. Its razor sharp talons gripped him with precision without causing him any harm. Suddenly, they were airborne.

The ground was no longer beneath his feet. In fact, the territory that was once overwhelming to his size became smaller as he began to ascend in the grasp of the eagle. He was being handled gently as if he were the offspring of the eagle. There was an unspoken bonding happening. It was all done to further the race for higher consciousness. As soon as their height was at a maximum altitude, Sonny was able to see the entire grand scale of the artificial town. There was a huge patch of land used to erect such a project. The air became thin to him as he soared above. However, he felt secure in the eagle's grip.

After some time in flight, they began making their descend. The location was a place on the outskirts of another city. The eagle landed with precision in a wooded area of town. Delicately, it released the salamander.

The salamander wasted no time scurrying toward the inner perimeter of town. The creature stopped at a grassy patch. There it began to shutter as if the ground beneath it were shaking. Through involuntary convulsions, the salamander began taking on another shape. Its human presence began to formulate from out of itself. The sounds of moaning and grunting persisted during the process of the metamorphosis. Its digestive system had to adapt to the stretching while keeping the system operating. Within minutes, Sonny resumed his original appearance. What was so puzzling about the entire ordeal was that he was fully clothed. The reason for it was quite simple. During the molecular reconstruction, the clothes he wore were also broken down to their natural elements. Elements which coincided with Sonny's own molecular composition. The fibers of the clothing were made from natural cotton, making it possible to break down molecularly. Sonny was fully clothed in the same attire he adorned before the transformation. The process caused him paralysis for a moment. Sonny regained his mobility shortly afterward. He stood and headed toward the town.

39.

Sonny entered an internet cafe restaurant along the main boulevard. The outside traffic noise quieted abruptly as the front door closed. Inside was quiet. The delightful scent of cinnamon and coffee waft through the air. Sonny blinked successively in effort to adjust his eyes to the transitioning of outdoor light to that in the cafe. The interior illumination of the cafe was dim. It illuminated a soft mellow light. Such lighting was easy on the eyes when viewing computer screens. There were people sitting at tables, booth seats, and counters. Patrons were silently working on their computers. Some were editors, writers, and free lancers. Some held positions as teachers, others were from other professions. Sipping hot beverages and working on text documents was the norm. Sonny ordered a beverage and found an unoccupied workstation. He sipped on Swiss

Mocha as he logged onto the social network. He entered the website address angreab@gmail.com. Moments later, the screen changed graphically. He began typing his message onto the screen.

***

The adjacent town was called Proctor. It was a small county in Texas. It is there the two met. They sat across from one another in a motel room. Outside, the setting sun turned the sky a greenish-purple with a splash of orange. It was visually a majestical setting.

Andrea was dressed in a blue, cotton blouse. Her blue, stone washed, jeans matched perfectly. She stood and walked over to the single window and drew the curtain closed. Returning to the bed, she sat next to Sonny who didn't seem nervous.

"I'm glad that you made it out of there. I couldn't stand being part of the charades going on with your life. I want to know…." She hesitated for a moment. "No! I don't want to know how you managed to get out of there. More likely, I want to know exactly who and what you are?"

Sonny studied her eyes and demeanor. He detected sincerity and concern. He could feel the sexual attraction that emitted from her. The scent excited him. "This is what I know…." Sonny began to explain his entire heritage to Andrea. He left nothing obscured. Speaking frankly with her came naturally.

After the lengthy explanation, Andrea continued to keep eye

contact with Sonny. "Wow! That was some story. That explains the entire thinking of the program and why they used you for a study specimen. They want the complete DNA codes. It would allow them to control the shape changes that you have the ability to perform. No! I am glad I separated from them.

"Okay, what will you do?" asked Sonny

"I don't know, but I do know I will have to keep a low profile and stay under the radar. My problem is money. If I used my personal information, they will locate me."

"I have a solution." Sonny explained about the numbers in his head that held cash, only he couldn't remember Gertrude. "Andrea, things are changing within my body. I need to mate in order to survive. The urge is more than just a wanting or lusting. It's a need."

Andrea looked into his eyes sensing the sincerity of his words. She kissed Sonny passionately. Their tongues did a dance inside of one another's mouths. Fervent emotions existed between them. Andrea hastily began to undress Sonny.

Sonny was relieved at her aggressive willingness. She seemed to understand the dynamics of the situation and willfully wanted to participate. Without words they communed and began exploring one another's bodies. To Andrea, it was the most unusual encounter. She never experienced a more heightened, fervid, and passionate emotion. She was filled, and at the same instance she felt insatiable. Andrea opened up wide to receive Sonny into her being. A blissful state was reached. The forceful discharges left them both spent and exhausted.

Andrea lie next to Sonny. She looked in his eyes. The gaze was so intense, she felt she could see into his soul. "Do you know what this means?"

Sonny looked at her knowingly. He nodded his head. "Yes, it means you are a principle part of our survival. You are now in the balance of our evolution." Sonny noticed her facial expression turning to disappointment. "What? Did I say something wrong?" She shook her head. It dawned on him. Sonny gestured by smacking his forehead with the palm of his hand. The sound was pronounced. The gesture brought merriment to Andrea. "Oh, I get it! Please believe me, what I feel for you is real. To be honest, I don't know if it's love because I've never experienced the sensation. I do know I feel a closeness. I really like you."

Andrea felt the sincerity in his words. She began blushing. "I know what you mean. I feel the same way."

"Let me ask you something." Sonny sighed deeply. "Now that you know what I am, tell me something. What compels you to want to be with me?"

Andrea didn't answer right away. She chose her words carefully. "I didn't plan anything. It's like a knowing to be chosen to do something. Something that I have no idea about. To be truthful, I am scared shitless. I know fear is nothing but false emotions appearing real. So I don't give it much life. Where we go from here is a mystery to me."

"Okay, the money part is taken care of. I know I want to be with you. It won't be safe for us to be seen together."

"I am willing to take that chance."

"I'm not!" exclaimed Sonny. He shook his head as a gesture. "Not with the probability of an offspring being present. That is the purpose of my existence. It was the same for so many others before me." The two kissed passionately.

BOOK

TWO

ANDREA'S

JOURNEY

40.

Andrea headed north after deciding it was unsafe for her and Sonny to travel, or be seen together. She had no knowledge of his whereabouts at the moment. It was decided it was better that way.

Wilmington, Delaware is where she found herself. She rented a house on a cul-de-sac in a residential, sub-division area. She used a fictitious name and the money from the account that Sonny mysteriously held to memory. It was still unclear how he obtained the knowledge of the account.

Andrea settled into her new life. She knew the power the Department of Defense possessed. She realized she could be tracked at any moment. She remained under the radar. To keep herself occupied, she began writing an autobiography. Purchasing a laptop computer, Andrea began logging accounts of her early life. To receive inspiration, she journeyed outside and explore different locations in the area.

Andrea visited a national park. The natural setting and wildlife were soothing to her senses. She watched the birds soar above. The sounds of chirping and the delightful scent of the floral was exuberant. The ambiance inspired her to continue documenting her story. At times her mind drifted to Sonny. She hoped he was well and safe. She knew he experienced an awful ordeal with the Department of Defense.

Months passed pleasantly. Andrea sometimes awoke abruptly from missing Sonny. One particular morning she awoke feeling ill. She rushed to the bathroom. Her stomach was aggravated. Kneeling over the toilet, Andrea heaved. She began vomiting into the commode. Later that day, she visited a private hospital to get an examination. The results revealed she was pregnant.

Andrea was taken by surprise at the diagnosis although she expected it after having unprotected sex. She remembered being swept away by passion and desires. She remembered feeling Sonny's manly juice run deep into her being. Amber realized life would never be the same.

Andrea visited a national park. She found herself writing on her laptop. She reflected on her life and the future of her unborn baby. She tried to find a name that would be suitable for the baby. Not knowing the sex of the unborn child, she selected names from a male and female list on the internet. A strange phenomenon happened.

Andrea looked around to see she was surrounded by wildlife. They weren't aggressive. They were passively perched around her. She was startled momentarily. That feeling was short lived when she sensed they were there to assist. Suddenly, it dawned on her as to what was happening. She remembered what Sonny had explained. The encounters he had with the animals, and the fact that he could communicate with them telepathically. She tried, but it was no use. She didn't possess the same facilities.

That evening, Amber tried to make sense of the early part of the day. *'I think they were trying to communicate with me. I must find a way to break through to them. I'm sure they know I am carrying Sonny's baby.'* A notion struck as she began surfing the websites. She wanted to see if Sonny made contact by leaving a text message. Disappointed at not finding anything, she closed the laptop and prepared for an afternoon nap.

***

Minutes turned into hours. Hours turned into days. Days turned into weeks. Weeks turned into months. Andrea's stomach had protruded. The pronounced bulge caused her mobility to become impaired. It saddened her that she didn't know of Sonny's whereabouts.

Today, she sat in the wooded park feeding the squirrels and pigeons. The sunshine began to ascend over the park. People passed by enjoying the delightful weather. Andrea placed her laptop next to her tote bag. She retrieved more nuts and seeds from the bag. Her mind was engulfed in thoughts of Sonny's whereabouts.

Unaware of her surroundings, Amber was approached by a man dressed in a black, t-shirt, blue jeans, and sneakers. He approached her from her blind side. In a fluid motion, he zeroed in on her unattended laptop computer. Stealthily, he picked it up. He concealed it to his side as he walked back toward the way from which he arrived.

Andrea exhausted all the seeds and nuts she held in her hands feeding the birds. She glanced over toward where her laptop computer once was. It was gone. Feeling bewildered about the situation, she looked around to see if it fell or if someone picked it up. There was no one in the area close by.

The man in the blue jeans and black, t-shirt was excited about his new score. His mind calculated the earnings it would bring. Suddenly, two eagles descended from the heavens directly above. Simultaneously, they moved in harmony with each another. They converged on the man from different angles. One pecked his head with its sharp hooked beak as its razor-sharp talons scratched at his skin. The attack drew blood in the process before it flew away. The assault caught the man totally off guard. The other bird of prey flew directly into the man's left hand as it held a grip on the electronic device. Upon contact with the bird, the man released his grip. The laptop computer headed toward the grassy ground. Before impact, the bird's strong legs and sharp talons grasped the handle of the portable computer. Its wide, wing span flapped exuberantly in effort to carry the payload. With much strain, its flight path ascended with the laptop in its grasp.

"What the…" Before his words were expelled, the thief felt a sharp sting in his eyes. For a split second, he witnessed the flapping bird's wings, then he lost his vision. Everything became pitched black in one eye. Then darkness enveloped in the other eye. The thief was now sightless. The sound of fear and agony was all that was heard.

After puncturing the thief's eyes, the eagle flew away catching up with the other. The two birds were now perched on a bench, one on each side of Andrea.

At first, Andrea was shocked to see the birds. Then it became apparent they were her allies. She had no idea about what had transpired. Andrea felt she was spared grief. Seeing the temporarily missing laptop was baffling.

***

Time became nonexistent for Sonny. The fact that he had mated allowed him to know his time was near. Keeping a low profile, Sonny ventured west. He found himself in the sunny side hills of Venice, California.

Sonny spent endless hours at the beach. He felt compelled to be near the seashore. He found being close to the water soothing and therapeutic. He felt he belonged in the water with the other species.

Sonny was in a mediative state when two men wearing dark suits, dark sunglasses, and hard bottom shoes converged on him from behind. Instantly, he felt a sensation of knowing. The hairs on the nape of his neck rose. He opened his eyes to see the men standing on either side of him. Subconsciously, Sonny knew this day would come. It was a matter of when. Sonny open his eyes acknowledging the men. He knew who they were, and who had sent them. He didn't resist. He felt his mission was accomplished.

"Can you please come with us?" asked the agent to the right of him.

41.

Sonny awoke in a white, padded room. The bed was wide and firm. The room held a white, porcelain toilet, a stainless-steel table, sink, and cabinet. The room was windowless. Time ceased to exist. Sonny gazed around the unfamiliar surrounding. No clocks to be seen anywhere. Sonny focused on what led him to his predicament. As soon as he began to stir, the door opened. A man in a long, white, laboratory coat entered. He was middle-aged and clean shaven. He wore designer eyewear and walked slightly hunched. A stethoscope was worn around his neck. A nameplate was attached to his lapel. It read Dr Hendrix.

"How are you feeling?" asked the doctor.

"What are you doing to me?" Sonny tried to move. He felt restrictions on his limbs. The restraints were noiseless because they weren't chains. They were brown, leather straps with fuzzy sheep fur on the inner part that touched the skin.

"You don't remember? When you left, so did one of our trusted staff members. You know her as Ms Banks. There are records of you two conversing for lengthy periods of time. Can you tell us what that was about?" Sonny didn't answer. He stared up at the off-white ceiling and the four foot fluorescent lighting fixture. Since the room was windowless, the only light in the enclosure was being artificially generated. "I'll take your silence as an omission."

"What do you want from me?"

"I'll tell you. We've invested a fortune in you. We hoped to examine your true potential on a molecular level. We know you have mutant genes. How? We are still baffled. You are a freak of nature that sparked our curiosity. So far, the money we've invested verses the results are unbalanced. You're going to perform for us if you want to live."

"I have nothing to fear. There is nothing you can do that can change my legacy."

"Legacy? What legacy? What do you think this is? A negotiation? Well, it's not." The technician turned and walked toward the locked stainless-steel cabinet. Opening a drug cache, he retrieved a syringe and a small clear bottle. The bottle was labeled with miniaturized lettering. He approached with the two items in hand. Slowly, he inserted the needle into the rubber sealed bottle of clear fluid. Working the plunger, he allowed the liquid to fill the syringe cylinder. Stopping at the desired amount, he proceeded to insert the needle into Sonny's restrained arm. Sonny tried to flail, only it was to no avail. The technician continued working effortlessly. Moments later, Sonny's body went limp as the fluid traveled through his bloodstream.

A series of test were performed. Now that the project was exposed to Sonny, to use evasive measures would be fruitless. A spinal tap was performed without the use of a pain masking drug. They didn't want to alter his chemical molecular structure. Sonny endured excruciating pain. He called out in agony fruitlessly. No one answered his call. Periodically, a staff member would appear to check his vitals. To them it was a hurried effort to find the information they needed before the inevitable would come to Sonny.

Sonny remembered going to the library in prior times. He was attracted to the religious section. He was drawn by the vagueness of the subject matter. Not fully understanding the entire concept, he recognized it dealt with believing in the unknown. He came across another interesting prominent character that seemingly was the nucleus to the story. His name was mentioned as Christ Jesus. For some strange reason, Sonny's mind referred to the time when Jesus Christ was made to suffer. He was able to relate the story to his own situation. He, also like Jesus, called aloud to the heavens.

Soon afterward, Sonny was brought out of his reverie by the sound of a key placed into the lock cylinder. He heard the cylinder being turned and the latch bolt released. The door opened. A female doctor entered. She was an attractive woman. She wore a long, white, laboratory coat. Her full figure was outlined through the garment. Her face was without makeup. Her stern facial demeanor and taut lips wouldn't allow her to smile. Her hooded eyelids were distinctive. The lady's face was expressionless. Sonny noticed one flaw to her facial appearance. He noticed she blinked excessively. A nameplate hung on her lapel. It read Dr Wiggins.

"How are we?" Sonny watched her vague expression. He automatically sensed danger. He didn't respond to her question. "Okay, I'll take the silence for a not-so-good answer. Let's see what we can do about that." Her voice was calm. She removed the catheter, then the intravenous tubes from his wrist. Next, she removed the sensory pads that monitored his vitals from the different locations on his body. The last thing she relieved Sonny from was the leather ties used to restrain his limbs.

"Why are you being so nice? What more do you want from me?"

"Actually, we're finished. I think we have all the information we need from you."

"Which is?" She didn't respond. "Let me ask you something. Are you religious? Are you familiar with the Bible?"

The question sparked her curiosity. "Yes I am."

"Do you believe what's written in it and what it stands for?"

Dr Wiggins answered hesitantly. "Yes, I am aware of the scriptures. I would like to say I do believe it."

"I've read about the life of Jesus. It seems to me it is generally acknowledged that killing him was a mistake. Then, why is it that we still continue to make those same misjudgments of others?"

"So, are you comparing yourself to Jesus Christ?"

"Jesus preached equality for all. Let's just say that I too understand the concept of the dogma more than others. I feel I too am a living person and deserve to live unhindered by others because of their lack of understanding."

After checking in with Sonny, Dr Wiggins returned to her office to log in the data. Her last encounter left a lingering thought about ethical morals. *'He does have a valid point but progress is inevitable with humans.'* A deep sigh followed her thought process.

Time passed, more test were performed. Sonny never experienced the threshold of pain he was undergoing. To relieve the sensation, he allowed his mind to drift. It always seemed to travel to the same place, to Andrea. He didn't know her exact whereabouts. That was a choice that they decided would be best. He could feel her presence right beside him. He sensed her existence, but not her location. Sonny knew time was nearing a complete evolution for his existence. He also understood the sole purpose for being. His cognition traveled forward to the present. His previous thoughts brought about a warming smile. He knew everything from that point onward was meaningless to the survival of his kind. He knew his mission was accomplished, a complete success. Closing his eyes, he produced a smile.

42.

After registering under a pseudonym, Andrea sat in the waiting room in a private hospital. She wanted to keep her personal life discreet even though she realized hiding from the Department of Defense was next to impossible. Andrea thought she had entered into labor. After being prepped and rushed into the operating room, she learned she had arrived prematurely. She was made to sit in the waiting area until her vaginal canal opened more centimeters. The waiting room was upscale. It held comfortable seating that included an entertainment center and amenities of a fine dining facility. Andrea craved a hot chocolate beverage. She ordered and returned to her table. She sipped on her beverage as her mind continued to plague her with thoughts. The pressure of uncertainty enveloped her being. Her mind was displaced to different scenarios she experienced.

Andrea's college years came into focus. She remembered taking her first job offering at the Department of Defense. She was placed in the research department. She remembered being asked to participate in a project while given only partial information into the ongoings of the work. She recalled being told the information was on a need-to-know basis. Then, she met Sonny. There were silent whispers from other staff members who knew what he was. Instead of being afraid and watchful as others were, Andrea became intrigued. Unexpectedly, she was returned from her daydream by excruciating pain in her stomach. The baby was getting restless. *'Okay, it's time to come out.'* She wanted it to be over. The pain at times was unbearable. She was also anxious to see the resemblance of the child along with its health factor.

***

Sonny awakened earlier than usual. Instinctively, he felt an eerie sensation. He sensed a change. Two attendants entered the room. Both men were muscularly built. Both men wore white shirts and white pants. Nameplates were attached to their shirt pockets. Keys jingled from a key ring on one of the men's belt. The men moved methodically with purpose and a sense of urgency.

Sonny was still restrained in his bed as he had been since his capture. The men were on both sides of the bed looking down at him. Simultaneously, they released the wheel locks to the bed. They began wheeling him out of the room into the well lit corridor. The hallway was spacious in width and length. The white, tile floors were highly polished. The walls were also bright. Everything looked uniform and clean.

Sonny spotted cameras as they passed. He noticed there weren't anyone present in the hall. He raised his head as high as he could above the pillow. He had to strain to make that happen. A sense of urgency overwhelmed him. "Where are you taking me?" There was no reply. No conversation ensued between him and his captors.

43.

The director of the research at the Department of Defense, along with two other well dressed gentlemen, sat in a conference room. The office was tastefully designed. The polished, mahogany table held stainless-steel water pitchers and crystal glasses. Some of the glasses were filled with water. The meeting had been ongoing for some time to determine if funding for Project Chameleon would continue or be terminated.

Mr Carmine, the director, stood in front of the group. He spoke from a podium. He was a man of tall stature; he was well dressed and neatly groomed. His only physical flaw was the spectacles he wore held thick lenses that hung on the tip of his aquiline nose.

"It sounds to me gentlemen you are at a snag in the road. No more useful data is being obtained. Is that so?" His eyes scanned the audience.

"I would like to say it's slow development," said a member.

"The longer we sustain this operation the easier the information we've obtain can become compromised. It won't be the first time. Remember gentlemen, you do realize what that could do to us."

"I understand. Remember, we have enough information to make a clone."

"We don't know if the clone will produce the same properties as the archetype." The statement was from one of the research technicians across the table. The conversation went back and forth from the supervisor and the others to the point that tension ensued amongst them. The topic was sensitive.

The director interjected. "Okay gentlemen, since we cannot come to an agreeable decision on this matter, I will decide." He examined the document on the table in front of him. "We will discontinue this program after a frontal lobotomy is performed. I am really interested to see the information it will reveal."

"The procedure can leave him vegetable-like or worst, kill the subject."

"Doesn't matter." The director sighed deeply. "The decision has been made. This meeting is adjourned gentlemen."

44.

The waiting room temperature was sweltering. Andrea found breathing difficult. She felt the baby stir inside her womb. Suddenly, the room began to spin. She stood abruptly. Andrea felt her blood pressure drop drastically. Andrea became nauseated. She became disoriented. Darkness engulfed her being.

Inside of the operating room, Andrea was positioned with her legs in stirrups. Her body was numb to the pain of natural childbirth. A pain relieving drug coursed through her veins. This was done through an intravenous drip tube that was located in her right wrist. Her mind drifted from reality to fantasy. She found it difficult to distinguish one from the other. Andrea knew that she was about to give birth. Not knowing the gender of her offspring was suspenseful.

Initially, she wanted it to be a genuine surprise. Deep inside, a girl is what she wished for. *'As long as it's healthy I will be happy.'* The entire ordeal left her exhausted. With her vision blurred, Andrea saw silhouettes of people moving about in front of her. Voices of people conversing was audible. She wasn't able to make out what they were saying. Her brain was acting too slow to decipher the phonetic tones.

Suddenly, pressure was felt in her stomach. Andrea knew something significant was happening. Something that would change her life, and the world as she knew it. *'It's time.'*

***

Sonny was restrained in an upright position. He sat on a special cushioned seat. His head was held in place by a modified brace. The apparatus ensured that the patient's head didn't move during the delicate surgery. The front lobotomy procedure was underway. It was thought by the researchers the act would control the electrical impulses that triggered the shape changes in Sonny's molecular structure. To everyone's thinking, the nerve in that region of the brain was used as a power charge, a detonator to quick start an episode. It was the only piece of the puzzle that truly baffled them. All the data obtained in the past was useless without the source of power.

Under heavy medication, Sonny sat motionless. A gaping hole was in the left hemisphere of his brain. A probe was attached to a camera. The surgeons were able to see a wide angle view to perform the delicate task. A graphic signal was channeled to a house monitor in the room. With the monitor, three surgeons worked methodically on the task at hand. Blood letting was very minimal. The blood that did drip was being absorbed by blotters.

***

Although she was heavily medicated, Andrea felt the pain associated with the emergence of her baby. Her vision was limited as the medication impaired her movement. Suddenly, the sound of a shriek emitted into the room. It was the cry of life from her newborn.

***

The surgeons were about to perform an excision on a piece of tissue from Sonny's brain. Suddenly, a strange phenomenon happened. Everyone in the room was in pure astonishment. The sudden shock of what was being visualized was unbelievable. The entire room quieted abruptly. The only sound that emitted in the bright, sterile environment were beeps that reverberated from the vital readings on the monitors. A loud piercing alarm resounded from the electrocardiograph monitor. The signal alerted the patient's heart was in distress. Red lights flashed across the monitor.

"Get the defibrillator!" shouted the head surgeon. "Get me 20 cubic centimeters of adrenaline. Stat!" The order was spoken sharply. Staff members went into action to save Sonny.

Very little, if any knowledge about what was taking place was known by the staff. A nurse handed the head surgeon the portable defibrillator. The device was rectangular in design, the size of a standard brick with two paddles connected by coiled wires. Sonny was attentively placed in a horizontal position. Careful measures were used in efforts not to upset the gaping hole in his head. His open gown exposed his hairless chest. A lubricant was placed on his chest and on the paddles.

"Set?" asked the head surgeon. He referred to the technician.

"Set."

The surgeon touched the two paddles together creating a surge of current. He applied the paddles to both sides of Sonny's chest. The electrical burst caused Sonny's body to jolt upward. Afterward, all attention went to the monitor. All eyes were watching the graphic lines. There was no change in activity.

"He's still experiencing palpitations," said the head surgeon. The process was repeated. The results were the same. He turned to face the registered nurse. "Nurse." His voice held a hint of desperation. It bothered him greatly to lose a patient. *'There will be no dying on my watch.'* He gestured to the nurse to hand him the next application to the task. The nurse was at the ready. She handed him a syringe filled with a clear liquid substance.

Just as the surgeon was about to insert the needle into Sonny's heart a miraculous phenomenon occurred. Right before everyone's eyes, Sonny began dematerializing. Openmouthed and standing aghast, the head surgeon mindlessly continued holding the syringe in his hand. His hands became unsteady. As his hands trembled, perspiration emitted through his pores. Beads of salty liquid glided down his forehead past the clear plastic facial mask that he wore for protection.

The others in the operation room began to exit in a hurried manner. The head surgeon apprehensively took it all in. Sonny knew it was time. He'd never experienced the feeling, but instinctively he realized the sensation was inevitable. He didn't try to fight the awareness. Multiple scenes from the past flickered across his mind. Some of the images were recognizable, a lot of them weren't. He recollected seeing his ancestor using her own body as a shield so that they could survive. It was the ultimate sacrifice, the giving of ones's own life for another. Unrecognizable images of people appeared. He didn't know the significance of it all. Sonny embraced everything that was happening. Pain no longer existed. His vision changed. He was able to see things in their natural essence. The head surgeon's image was viewed by Sonny as a blurred vapor. Haze hovered in front of him. Sonny was no longer bound by the restraints of man. He was no longer on the plane of the physical.

Unseen, a vacuumed force began pulling him upward into the ethereal. The force originated in the celestial's outer core of space. The force became a strong suction that pulled Sonny's essence toward it. He allowed himself to be taken willingly. All that remained in the aftermath was the hospital gown he once adorned.

***

As the newborn emerged, the doctors saw the abnormality in the infant. Everyone was quiet as they gazed in disbelief.

Andrea knew something was wrong. "W-what is it? What's wrong with my baby?" Her voice was hysterical.

"Please calm down. Your son is in good hands. He's alive." The nurse tried to comfort her.

The other doctors placed the baby to the side, away from Andrea's view. As they examined the crying infant, they discovered his feet and hands were webbed. His eyes were that of a reptile. His skin was that of a human being. Not wanting her to see the child and go into shock, they avoided giving her visual contact.

"Let me see my baby."

"Soon, we must prepare him for testing as a precaution."

"Precaution from what?" Andrea began to stir, trying to get out of her position in the stirrups. Her stomach and birth canal were sore.

"You'll have to calm down. Everything will be all right. You will be reunited with your child in a moment," said the registered nurse. Andrea was injected with a tranquilizer. The drug took effect immediately. She calmed quickly. Andrea became unconscious.

BOOK

III

EIGHTEEN

MONTHS

LATER

45.

UNITED STATES DEPARTMENT OF DEFENSE
CONFERENCE ROOM/A
9:27 AM

A heated discussion had been underway for over a hour. There were four men sitting around the high-tech glass table. The table top was a digital monitor that could display huge graphic images for discussion. The surface was also equipped with touch screen technology allowing the user manipulation. Three of the men wore pristine, dark colored suits. They were well groomed, high ranking officials. One of the four men seated at the table displayed prominence. His projecting image was that of importance mainly because he was dressed in a military uniform. There were an array of metals worn on the right breast of his uniform. The metals were of different shapes. There were also multi-colored ribbons adorned along side them. The five stars on the lapel foretold his standing as a general in the armed forces.

"Gentlemen, we are not getting anywhere this way," exclaimed the director. His voice rose over the cacophonous sounds of everyone trying to get their point across simultaneously. "We need to vote on the course of action."

"I say we continue to use the Homeland Security Act to buy more time," stated the man in a dark suit. He was from the Homeland Security branch.

"I say we separate them permanently." The owner of that statement held up his hand as he waved away the disappointing stares of the others. "I know it sounds horrible but sooner or later she will have to be released with her child. She's done nothing wrong. We don't know exactly how long this research will take. Wouldn't you agree it would be better if the lab boys didn't have a deadline? If the child is parentless, then he will become a ward of the state. It would be easier for us to obtain the rights of adoption. This time we can do it right because we have a subject from birth. Monitoring will be so much easier."

The room quieted down. All eyes were on the General. They contemplated on what was said. Everyone knew it was a hard decision to have to make. They agreed it had to be done.

"Okay, it's a done deal."

***

Andrea's mind was constantly clouded. Visions drifted of surreal images. Although she was heavily medicated, Andrea was able to muster the cognitive capacity to know she had just given birth. The timing of the event was obscured. In reality it happened more than 18 months ago. Drugs were being fed to her constantly via intravenous methods.

Never having the chance to hold and bond with her newborn child, Andrea was able to feel her offspring's existence. The encounter was bizarre. Her baby's gender was ever known, only the life force of the offspring. Suddenly, a chilling sensation occurred to Andrea. She felt an external force enter her being. The experience caused an involuntary shiver to control her body.

Two men entered her quarters. Both were of different physical stature. They were dressed identically with laboratory coats and name tags on their lapels. One carried keys, the other carried a chart board. They entered the room noticing the patient was wide awake.

Andrea's mind was too unsteady to make out the distinction of the men. Their faces meant nothing. She fought hard through muddled thoughts and visions. Andrea faintly heard conversation ensuing.

"Let's get this over with quickly," stated the staff member with keys jingling in his hand. The sound of the keys resonated in the quiet room. He placed them in his other hand in order to choose the appropriate one. Locating it, he headed toward the stainless-steel cabinet. Using the chosen key, he unlocked the cache of drugs. Selecting a specific vial, he retrieved it along with a syringe. He approached the bed where Andrea lie restrained. A drip bag with clear liquid flowed through a transparent, plastic tube into her arm.

The staff member holding a chart board glanced at his watch. He began jotting information onto a form that was attached to the chart board. "Okay, you may begin."

The man with the vial and syringe held the bottle up toward the fluorescent lighting fixture to enable a better view. After examining the bottle, he inserted the needle into the rubber seal on top of the vial. The label on the small vial read POTASSIUM BROMIDE. He withdrew the plunger and filled the syringe cylinder with a clear liquid. He stopped at 40 cubic centimeters. He injected it into an attachment connected to the drip feed. The liquid mixed with the other transparent liquid. The mixture headed directly toward Andrea's bloodstream.

Andrea sensed something detrimental was occurring. She couldn't determine the exact threat. Her mind seemed separated from her body. Her body began an independent quest for survival. Andrea began feeling an eerie sensation. Unknowingly, a trait from Sonny's genes had entered her body during copulation. Slowly her body began to dematerialize in effort to beat the toxic chemical that raced toward her bloodstream.

An unexplainable race against time was underway. An uncharted territory was being discovered. Andrea's body began to react on its own will. Her entire metabolism and chemical composition began transforming into an unnatural element. Her body began oxidizing with the help of the atmosphere. Metabolically, it was at an accelerated pace on the outer appearance. A dematerialization had begun.

The potassium bromide traveled down the transparent tube. The toxic substance was set to mix with the plasma at five drops per minute. At that pace, the potassium bromide would begin its paralyzing effect within minutes of entering the bloodstream. The muscles would be the first to be affected. Under certain doses, the deadly chemical was known to cause involuntary convulsions. In moderate doses, it would affect the brain and the muscles almost simultaneously. The subject would not suffer long before the inevitability of death was upon the patient. Andrea felt her breath become depleted. For a moment, the feeling of suffocation overwhelmed her. The sensation was compared to being submerged under water and being deprived of oxygen. She was momentarily panic-stricken. She began to relax as a bright, light illuminated and warmed her inner being. She heard her name called invitingly.

The technicians stood in pure astonishment. Bewildered, they couldn't believe what they were witnessing. They stood stark still as they witnessed the paralytic effect the startling emotion held on them. They were in shock. Watching the subject slowly disappearing was unnatural to their concepts. There was nothing they could do but remain still in disbelief. The law of reasoning failed to exist. They realized after making the necessary report of what happened, chances were they would likely be committed for psychiatric evaluations. Hopefully, the surveillance system in the room had recorded the entire sequel. All that was left of the patient now was the gown she once adorned.

"Man, I don't believe this!"

"Neither do I. Come on, we have to report this."

46.

UNITED STATES DEPARTMENT OF DEFENSE
TESTING FACILITY
BLDG-G/AREA-B
10:27 AM

The long awaited results of Project Chameleon was underway. A prototype was finally completed and ready for presentation. The facility was spacious with a heightened ceiling. The area was the size of an aircraft hanger. The floor was polished tile. Men and women dressed in white, jumpsuits with large lettering on the back moved about the facility methodically. Bold letters on the jumpsuits displayed governmental insignia embossed in black.

A group of high ranking officials were seated adjacent to an elevated platform. On stage, a slide projector and other presentational tools were set up. A huge screen was on display. A bare-chested man wearing shorts sat in a chair perfectly still. His body was well maintained. His skin was pale with slight splotches of blemishes. His freckles were prominent. He sat in a chair motionless. His eyes were closed as if he were meditating. The presentation had begun. There was a historic discussion into the origin of the project. Also, the inside look into the mindset of the idealist. Soon, what everyone came to see had began to unfold.

"Ladies and gentlemen, I am proud to present to you a new phenomenon. One that will change your world forever and the way you view it. Recalling the adage 'let the action speak for itself'." Applauses erupted in the area. When the ovation subsided, the speaker continued. "Through ultimate research, this is what we've achieved. Mind you, this could be the new generation of soldiers and warfare." He nodded to his associate seated in the chair.

The seated bare-chested man wearing shorts stood. He didn't speak. He seemingly was in deep concentration. His eyes were closed. He stood with his legs spaced apart and his arms extended outward. He resembled a magician doing a parlor trick with the use of smoke screens and mirrors. The subject's skin began to morph. Everyone was wide-eyed and in awe. They were unprepared for the event. A discordant hum erupted.

The subject's skin continued to evolve. His once bare skin was now layered in a hard shell. The color was that of hunter-green. The protective coating expanded upon his entire body, including his face and head.

The speaker did something unexpected. His action caught everyone off guard. The show of amazement was displayed on everyone's face. The moment resembled being in a carnival attraction where a woman was turned into a gorilla. Unexpectedly, she breaks free from her confinement. The frightened crowd heads for the exits. This phenomenon was real. The speaker retrieved a semi-automatic, 9mm, handgun from a concealed holster. His movement was fluid and unanticipated by the spectators.

PLOP!

PLOP!

PLOP!

Three loud explosions, along with fire and smoke, ejected from the weapon. The action erupting the already volatile setting. It gained everyone's attention. The act was surprising and deafening. Everyone in the area was taken by surprise. Even the security teams were alerted. They were seen unholstering their own firearms and standing at the ready position awaiting further orders.

The general's face was stern on the exterior. He proudly smiled mentally at the accomplishment of using the element of surprise. He had credited it to the reason for his success in the armed forces. The projectiles ejected from the 9mm, semi-automatic, handgun was with much force and accuracy. The trajectory was aimed directly toward the subject's body hitting him twice in the chest and once in the head. The subject's body jolted from the powerful impact. That was the extent of the aggressive maneuver. The subject was unscathed. The subject stood stark still on the platform facing the audience as if nothing transpired. He was covered in a foreign reptilian armor. After the initial shock subsided, applauses resumed.

"You see ladies and gentlemen, although it's been a long drawn out process, Project Chameleon is alive and bearing fruit as you have just witnessed. This is just the beginning. We are on the cutting edge to making the world safer with indestructible weapons. Soldiers will no longer have to die senselessly on the battlefield." More applauses ensued.

The director and other high-ranking officials sat in the front row feeling proud of the decision to continue Project Chameleon.

47.

More than a decade had passed since the breakthrough of Project Chameleon. So many new discoveries and concepts had arisen thereafter. The technology was safeguarded using high security measures.

Little, if any actual knowledge of the ones responsible for the research was known. It was esoteric by design. The newborn was taken away from his biological mother at birth. He held so much promise for the project's success. His DNA was cross-matched and interfused with other similar genes. The same process was done with other compounds to make new discoveries. Everyone realized they were treading on unchartered territories. The subject was not given a standard nomenclature, he was referred to as X-12. He was raised artificially in chambers designed to resemble actual life for species of his kind. Special programs were designed and filtered to him through mediums of all kinds. An intense regimen of psychological monitoring and thought enhancement programs went into the development of the subject.

X-12 grew into a fine young man. His hair was jet-black and curly. His webbed features retracted to normality over the years. His eyes took on a soft, greenish hue. His once abnormal features had corrected themselves automatically. He was now a handsome young boy. The older he became, the more he resembled someone of African origin. His full lips and bulbous nose was that of his great-great grandparents. Not knowing his history, X-12 didn't question his true existence. He was raised around technicians that probed and tested him frequently. Not knowing what normality meant, X-12 thought his lifestyle was the way life was meant to be. He wasn't hungry, sad, nor mistreated. The technicians displayed genuine concern for his wellbeing. He became exceptionally friendly with a certain research technician. His name was Dr Webster.

Dr Webster was a Scandinavian man who was brought to the states at a very young age. His father was a bio-chemist. He used plant life, along with other living organisms, to find cures for diseases. He was successful in most cases. Dr Webster was given his first chemistry set around the time he first learned to speak. Remembering compounds and their molecular value was natural for him.

When Dr Webster was born, the same systematic programming was implemented toward his learning. Dr Webster did exactly as his father. After gaining his doctorate degree in biological chemistry, he began working for the United State's government.

Working in the Bio-Chemical Research Department laboratory, he was finally given an important project. Combining DNA from X-12 with human cells first presented itself as nearly impossible. An idea dawned on him. The sequence of introducing the elements was the key. He really grew fond of X-12. Actually, he didn't like calling him that. Dr Webster was so engrossed in his work, that he'd never taken the time to find a companion to raise a family with.

When X-12 came along, he began to put an affectionate attachment to him. *I'll name him Marcus,'* Dr Webster began secretly teaching Marcus different disciplines. Amazingly, Marcus held an aptitude for the study and advanced faster than expected. The doctor shared intellectual books on psychology and social behavior. The two became very close. He even taught him to play chess.

One day at a meeting, the doctor was questioned about his association with the subject X-12. Dr Webster responded by letting the supervisors know it was a healthy relationship for the sake of the research. He had gained the ultimate goal, the confidence of X-12.

***

A meeting was called the next day with the department heads. The conference room held key figures from the armed forces and governmental agencies. There were men and women in attendance.

Some where jotting notes, some listened. A few of the personnel were dressed in high-ranking uniforms. Others adorned civilian clothing.

"Ladies and gentlemen, I am not going to stand up here and give an extended lecture on the history of the security of this great government. We all know there are eminent threats that exist. Some are within our very borders. What I came to tell you is, Project Chameleon maybe under cyber-attack." A dissonant hum erupted in the room. Simultaneous whispers reverberated in the enclosure. "Important top secret information could have been compromised by hackers from abroad or domestically."

"Do we have a source of interception?" asked a uniformed man.

"We believe it's North Korea."

"The dirty bastards!" shouted another person dressed in civilian clothing.

"So what is the proposed plan of action?" asked a well dressed man wearing a dark suit and black tie.

"First, we gather all the information to one source. Then we terminate all the evidence to deny this project ever existed. Then, we go after who is responsible."

Dr Webster listened. He felt disheartened. Just the thought of placing Marcus in harms way was unthinkable. He devised a plan of his own. He raised his hand to speak. "What is the timeline we're looking at?"

"Worst case scenario? I'll say three months tops."

48.

Dr Webster worked expeditiously to do what was needed. Lately, there was no time to spend with Marcus. That part saddened him but it was necessary. All of his spare time was spent in the laboratory under the microscopes and doing mathematical equations for biological formulas.

Marcus busied himself with studies and chores. He felt an emptiness because of Dr Webster's absence. He felt alienated and rejected. Marcus longed for the companionship for which he'd grown accustomed. He remembered their last encounter. *'I have a lot to do. When I am finished, I will tell you what you need to do. Then, we can be together always.'* Marcus continued with his studies. Curiosity crossed his mind periodically. He tried to make sense of the conversation. *'I hope he's not sick,'* he thought.

The weeks passed quickly. Dr Webster painstakingly worked around the clock on his private project. It was a race against time, and he'd won. He felt elated at that moment. He had created a culture and incubated it. The cells grew at an alarming rate of speed. Its cellular development was extraordinary. Within five weeks, the culture was full-grown. The outcome was a cloned figure of Marcus. The doctor was impressed with the task he accomplished. The figure was an exact replication. He was ecstatic over the results. *'Okay, phase one is complete. Now for the next phase.'*

***

Marcus was in his living compartment reading a book on social living. He was contemplating the dynamics that went into the interactions of the human species. He viewed it as a remarkable concept. A knock came to the door. He adverted his attention toward the door.

"Come in."

The door slowly opened. Dr Webster entered. He closed the door behind. He was dressed in his traditional white, laboratory coat. Marcus immediately noticed his tired and disheveled appearance. Weeks prior, dark circles had began to formulated under his eyes.

"Hey kiddo, got a minute?"

Marcus felt mixed emotions. He was happy to see his friend and at the same instance saddened by his appearance and elusive absence. An intense optimism had quickly formulated from within. "Sure, come in." Marcus shut the book he was reading. The book was closed with a sound that resonated with a dull thud. "Please have a seat."

Dr Webster sat on a chair adjacent to the bed. "I know we haven't spent much time together. Believe me it was necessary."

"For what?" retorted Marcus.

Dr Webster sighed deeply. He chose his words carefully. "The reason I haven't been around was because I've been trying to save you."

"Save me? Save me from what?"

"I want you to listen to me very carefully. There are things you don't know that you should. You were brought to this place for experimental purposes. You were programmed to believe what you see is reality. You were programmed to believe you are as normal as the others. The truth is you come from a lineage of a different kind. They have the information they sought, now they want to terminate the program. I can't allow that to happen." Marcus's facial expression displayed astonishment and confusion. "I want you to try to understand me. Your atomic molecular structure is different; you have the ability to shape change. You have the chemistry within to tap into it. It is triggered through your brain waves. Listen very carefully, this is what we're going to do...."

49.

It had been three weeks since their brief encounter. Marcus awoke abruptly. He was anxious from the anticipation of the forthcoming day. What was difficult to understand was the power he held within. At times he felt as a stranger in his own body. Finally, he tapped into what was told to him by Dr Webster. At first, the reasoning was foreign to his ears. It was as if the doctor was speaking an untranslatable language. The phonics seemed similar to ancient Latin.

Marcus went through the day doing his normal activities while teetering on the edge for what was to come. He checked the time from the clock on the wall. He headed into the bathroom.

***

Dr Webster completed his daily routine in the laboratory. He found two technicians to help push a gurney through the corridor.

"Is X-12 ill Dr Webster?" asked a technician. He wore a white, laboratory coat with his security badge on the lapel.

"Just routine testing. He had to be sedated. It will wear off in a couple of hours."

"Poor kid."

The technicians helped wheel Marcus into the room. They exited without anymore questions. Dr Webster feigned the act of adjusting Marcus's medications. As soon as the technicians left the room, Dr Webster went into action. He headed directly into the bathroom. He glanced around the room searching the floor for something. Finding it, he picked it up and placed it in his pocket. Dr Webster exited the building nonchalantly.

***

The routine ritual of exiting the building was underway. To Dr Webster it felt nerve-wracking. He went from the decontamination chamber to the locker room. Afterward, he headed toward his office. From there it was to the elevator, then through the checkpoint station. It was there when his emotions began to go haywire. Although he was familiar with the procedure and the people associated with it, he felt self-conscious. As he was about to step through the scanner, Dr Webster felt as if his heart would explode. He began perspiring profusely. He thought his heartbeat could be heard from outside his body. Clearing the machine seemed timeless. The act of retrieving his personal possessions from the trays was another nerve-wracking event. Finished, he headed for the exit.

"Dr Webster!"

The voice was strong and commanding. The doctor was startled. He stopped in his tracks. *'Maybe they're onto me.'* His thought was convincing. *'Maybe I can run toward the exit and make a dash to the car before they nab me.'* He knew it would be impossible. Dr Webster turned toward the sound of the voice.

"You forgot your cellphone."

Dr Webster didn't realize he was holding his breath. He released his airflow in the form of a sigh. He smiled nervously. Beads of sweat gathered on his forehead. He returned to the security station to retrieve the device.

The guard looked at him closely with concern. "Dr Webster is everything all right? You don't look so good."

"Yes Pat, I'm just tired from being overworked. My stomach hasn't been too well today." He accepted the cellphone and placed it in his jacket pocket. "Thank you for your concern." The doctor continued heading toward the exit.

Carrying his shoulder bag, along with his attache case in his left hand, Dr Webster placed his key in the lock cylinder of his vehicle. He turned the key and listened to the distinctive sound of the lock mechanism. He entered the vehicle. Dr Webster drove toward the heavily secured front gate.

As he approached the gate, he saw two familiar armed security guards. They carried MP-4, automatic weapons. The short stock of the weapons looked menacing.

"Hi Tom. Hi Brady," greeted Dr Webster. He tried willfully to keep a calm composure.

"Hi Dr Webster."

"Good night Dr Webster," greeted the guards simultaneously. Soon after the security gate was lifted, Dr Webster exited the premise.

As soon as the doctor cleared the gate he headed toward the flow of traffic. Suddenly, in the distance a faint sound of an alarm resounded. The noise added to his anxiety. In his rear view mirror he could see the guard dashing toward the compound. He pulled off into the flow of traffic. He blended in with the other motorist.

50.

"How could this have happened?" exclaimed the director of operations. He, along with other officials, and three armed guards rushed toward X-12's quarters. They were fearful that something had gone wrong. A worrisome thought entered the director's mind. A relief worker entered X-12's room and checked the bed chart. Puzzled, he found the bedside chart board didn't have any entries. They knew it wasn't Dr Webster's character to forget. He was a serious-minded person and repetitious in his routine. X-12 was his project and he took enormous pride in it.

The group entered the room to find X-12 asleep. They glanced around the room. Everything seemed to be in order. Nothing appeared to be disturbed. They decided to awaken X-12. When the director gazed into X-12's eyes, they were completely jet-black. There were no white in his orbs. It was a sign what they were looking at wasn't X-12. It was a close resemblance, an imitation. They realized it was a cloned figure of him. During the reproduction stages the eyes were the last to develop. Immediately, they notified headquarters about the situation. The director knew heads would roll. He truly hoped his was spared.

***

A thought emerged as Dr Webster drove along the freeway. Frustrated, he slammed his hands on the steering wheel. He was upset at his own forgetfulness. It occurred to him he neglected to log in his time and data with the patient. Quickly, he detoured his route from going to his house. He exited at the nearest opening. Dr Webster became aware of his actions and the serious consequences involved. The fact that he didn't put much thought into his plan was evident. His mind was mainly trained on what he knew. The act of secretly creating a clone was a job in itself. The mere thought of having to terminate Marcus's life was enough for him to act. Although he placed his career and his entire life's work in jeopardy, there were no regrets. Dr Webster realized he had to figure something out. He glanced at the case that held Marcus in the form of a small creature that resembled a salamander. He was able to fit it into his case. Marcus was still, it was as if he were confident that his friend would figure things out.

'Think! Think!' Dr Webster steered the vehicle toward the nearest exit.

Just as the vehicle came toward a yield sign where the local traffic merged parallel, the sound of a police cruiser erupted. The vehicle headed directly toward them at an alarming rate of speed. Dr Webster's heart skipped a beat. *'This is it!'* He felt as if his heart would jump from his chest. The patrol car enlarged in size as it neared. The patrol car was now inches from Dr Webster. He was panic-stricken. Miraculously, he noticed the cruiser continued moving onward. The driver paid no attention to him. As the patrol car sped pass, Dr Webster began to relax. It was then that he realized he was holding his breath.

HONK!

The sound startled him. It was a motorist behind him impatiently awaiting for him to move onward. Through his rearview mirror he was able to see the driver was irritated due to his lack of movement. He could tell from the motorist's body language, the driver was ranting and raving in the confinement of his vehicle. Dr Webster increased his speed to blend with the other motorists.

He steered the vehicle toward an industrial area in the city. The scenery changed drastically. Government facilities and residential housing were nonexistent in the area. All that existed were warehouses, junk yards, landfills, and public storages. The latter is what the doctor pursued.

The vehicle stopped in front of a huge storage lot. Other vehicles and people were in the area using the rented storage spaces. The doctor opened a compartment. Inside was filled with boxes and cases of laboratory equipment. It was things he collected over the years. He hoped one day to open his own practice. Rummaging through boxes, he found what he was looking for. He changed clothes. Afterward, he began taking things he thought would come in handy and placing them in a tote bag. He placed Marcus in the new carry bag using a tee shirt as a cushion. Dr Webster exited and headed toward the parking area. He detoured from the vehicle that he arrived in and entered into another. This one was a small sedan of German craftsmanship.

***

The Department of Defense Command Center was very active with personnel moving about. Some staff members were stationed at computer terminals. Some were monitoring satellite imaging equipment, while others commandeered the thermonuclear screens. There were personnel dressed in military uniforms, along side others dressed in civilian attire.

"Come on people! I want them found. They are not on the moon, they're right here on earth. If I can read the date on a nickel from three thousand miles above the earth, surely you can find two people." No one responded. They continued working at their stations. The director was agitated at how relaxed the security was in the Pentagon. "Okay, let's use time-lapse imaging against distance. It will at least give us a search radius."

One technician went to the blackboard and began drawing diagrams.

***

Knowing the capabilities of the Department of Defense, Dr Webster knew he had to act quickly and precisely. He was aware of their powerful imaging equipment located above the earth. He drove to a truck stop on Route 78. He took his carry bag along with him into the restroom.

The area was modern. It was equipped with state-of-the art sinks and toilets. No touch technology was in use. There were also showers, changing stations, other amenities of a quality hotel. There, he did what he could to create a deception.

Exiting the rest area while carrying the same tote bag was an elderly woman. She was adorned in blue jeans, brown blouse, and makeup. Her hair was honey brown. The doctor wore dark eyewear. The next phase of the escape plan would require precision and luck.

51.

"Okay people! They've been gone for nine hours. They should be in a jail cell right now and not roaming around the f**kin' streets! Did we get anything from the cellphone calls? His relative's data?" The director's anger was mounting. "I should know how many times he flushed the toilet by now. People let's go! This is why you're here." He snapped his fingers dramatically to emphasize his statement.

"Sir." A technician spoke. He was sitting behind a computer terminal. "His telephone isn't transmitting a signal. That probably means he has disconnected by breaking it because the device would still transmit when turned off."

The director began pacing the floor. Pensively, his mind was preoccupied with the task at hand. "Okay, Dr Webster." He was speaking aloud to no one in particular. "So, you want to play games?

Where would I go if I were on the run?" His question were more like statements to himself. No one answered. He stopped pacing. Spontaneously, he snapped his fingers as an idea occurred. "I want a picture sent out to all the agencies. I want the airports and Coast Guard notified. Also, put out a criminal search for him on the media. Say he's wanted for questioning in a murder." The director knew if he could attack the doctor's credibility it wouldn't be so easy for Dr Webster and Sonny to continue hiding. Law enforcement and civilians would be on the lookout. It would broaden the search capacity.

Armed with cash, the doctor went to visit the underground criminal world. He learned of it from a colleague in college. He visited a dimly lit pub on the south side of town. Armed with only a name, Dr Webster mentioned it to the bartender. The bartender was a slim man with hazel eyes and an aquiline nose. He wore a soiled apron around his waist. He studied the doctor's demeanor. Not feeling the doctor was suspicious or an eminent threat, he escorted the doctor to the rear of the shop through a doorway.

The room was a small confined space. An old-fashioned kitchen table was the only furniture in the middle of the room. Atop were liquor bottles and shot glasses. Toward the end of the room was photo equipment and computer equipment.

"Okay, I don't have all night. Do you have all the cash?" Dr Webster nodded nervously. "Good, I want you to stand over there. You can smile if you like it's your choice." The man swallowed a shot of liquid and began working.

One hour later, Dr Webster exited the pub with a new identification and new name. The depiction on the document was of a female. His next attempt would seal his fate.

52.

The Sea Devil bounced upon turbulent waves. The temperature in the region was warm and breezy. The wind came in from the southeast at 15 miles per hour. The sky was clear. There wasn't a cloud on the horizon. The massive fishing boat traveled 20 miles offshore in search of crabs.

Dr Webster, dressed in drag, sat below deck. His tote bag was near, only Marcus wasn't in it. Marcus had began morphing earlier back into his human anatomy. When the process was finished, he was totally exhausted.

The doctor kept close watch while he rested. The crew onboard were given orders to not interfere with him. The captain was paid well for his access on the ship.

When Marcus was fully recharged he awakened. He was famished beyond descriptive words. He was given clothing to wear and food to eat. Marcus devoured his food hastily. He was constantly reprimanded by the doctor to slow down. His thirst was also magnified due to the molecular change.

"Are we safe?"

The doctor nodded. "Yes we are, at least for the moment."

"Where are we? I smell salt."

"That's because we're out at sea. I paid the captain to take us to a neighboring border. We will sail in a small vessel from there. We should be good. How do you feel?"

"The encounter was beyond description. I can tell you this, it was a natural experience. Knowing I have this kind of power inside of me makes me question who I am. You know more about me than I know about myself. That's highly unusual. Wouldn't you say?"

The doctor began explaining to Marcus about his legacy again. He was patient because he knew it wasn't an easy story to digest mentally. Even to the doctor it sounded fictitious at times as he retold the story.

Three hours into the sail a loud horn erupted from above deck. The sound reverberated down below. A loudspeaker blared in the once serene atmosphere. The authoritative voice was mechanical. Orders were being given.

Down below, a knock came to the door. Dr Webster signaled for Marcus to hide. He opened the door partially, using his body as a shield to keep the intruder out. It was one of the crew members. His voice held a Spaniard accent.

"The captain said you will have to prepare for the ship to be boarded." He turned and retreated back upstairs to join the others.

Coast guard seamen were dressed in full battle uniforms on the deck. They carried intimidating weapons as they boarded the Sea Devil. They began checking identifications from the entire crew.

***

"I'll go up and see what I can do to hold them off. Meanwhile, I want you to change back."

"B-but I don't know if I can. I'm too nervous to concentrate."

"Just do it!" snapped the doctor. It was more of a command than a request. Frustrated, the doctor headed out of the door toward the upper deck.

On the upper deck, the crew were made to stand in line formation. Each person had their identification documents checked and verified. The doctor, dressed in drag, joined the group. He presented his fictitious documents. The process was slow and time consuming. His nerves were being tried and tested to capacity. After passing the initial check point, Dr Webster was alarmed at another occurrence being implemented. One of the soldiers held an electronic device in his hand. He pointed it at each person's face. The device emitted a tone. The soldiers went from person to person.

Sweat cascaded down the doctor's face. He recognized the device immediately. *'Oh my God!'* As soon as the guard neared, the doctor felt his heart rate soar. The soldier looked to him indifferently, mainly because he was told they were looking for a male and not an older woman. To the soldier's surprise, the device began to alarm. The doctor reacted quickly. He pushed the guard, who was not ready for the sudden confrontation. Being off balance, he fell backward. The doctor rushed toward the stairs leading below deck. As he darted, the sound of a shot rang out. He felt the wind from the velocity of the projectile as it rushed past his head.

Making it downstairs his adrenaline flowed freely. He pushed open the door expecting to search for a creature of some kind. To his disappointment, Marcus was still in human form.

"I-I couldn't-"

"Get down!" snapped the doctor. As soon as he cleared the room and headed for Marcus, two soldiers entered.

"Stop! Get on the ground! Now!" The commands were distinct and threatening.

The doctor shielded Marcus with his body. "Change Marcus! Change!" shouted the doctor. There was desperation in his voice.

The soldiers pointed their weapons. One of them used a two-way radio on his person. "We have them below." He spoke excitedly into the receiver. Spittle ejected from his mouth. Static erupted in the room from the transmission.

"You will not harm him!" Dr Webster lunged forward. Before he could do any harm to the soldiers, a loud blast erupted. Fire, smoke, and pain was all he experienced. Complete calm and darkness permeated his existence. Dr Webster's body fell to the hardwood floor. He was breathless and unmoving.

"N-nnooo!" shouted Marcus. He was completely absorbed in anguish. The sound was that of despair. With so much emotion running through his body and mind, something internal was triggered. His metabolism and molecular structure reacted violently. Instantly, his skin morphed with hardened scales. The hue of the scales were greenish-blue. The coating covered his entire body. During the transformation his muscle strength heightened.

PLOP!

PLOP!

The loud blast reverberated in the close confines. Fire and smoke erupted from the weapon's muzzles. Seeing his best friend lie motionless on the hardwood floor caused something inside of Marcus to explode. He had no control of it.

The projectiles ejected from the muzzles hit their intended mark with precision, only the velocity did nothing to penetrate the shield of scales on Marcus' body. The material shrouded his entire body. The deadly lead projectile fragmented upon contact with Marcus' body. Pure terror was displayed in the eyes of the soldiers. The men were astonished beyond belief at what they witnessed. The weapons trembled in their hands. Before they could regain composure, it was too late. From that moment forward, everything was a blur. All that was heard were screams of terror and pain.

Marcus lunged forward at lightning speed. The killing of the two soldiers was quick and easy. They folded under his touch like two rag dolls.

More soldiers entered through the threshold. Gunfire erupted. The barrage of bullets had no effect on the impregnable scales on

Marcus' body. The strange phenomenon was the projectiles reflected and fragmented upon contact with the armored shell. The impact was absorbed by the outer shell. Marcus repeated his action as he did with first two soldiers. They were no match for his speed and strength. Within moments, quietness and stillness was all that existed. His hearing and vision were heightened. Scanning the scene, Marcus sensed the threat was over. On a subconscious level his brain sent out a signal causing his body to retract. It was all done involuntarily. Marcus's body retracted to normal composition. It was a natural transition.

After the lightheadedness dissipated, Marcus stooped and picked up his best friend's lifeless body. The doctor's clothing was saturated in his own blood. Marcus felt a fervent anger arise deep within. He gave off an eerie yell that stemmed from anguish and despair. He saw the other crew members rush downstairs below deck. Marcus wasn't alarmed, he realized they had helped them.

Suddenly, the captain pushed through the crowd. He looked at the gruesome scene. His gaze stopped at Marcus.

"I didn't know there were two of you. You have to get off of this ship now!" He gave order for the others to clean up the scene. Marcus knew the man was in charge of the vessel.

The Coast Guard boat was abandoned and left to drift at sea while the Sea Devil sailed away. Marcus was in a life raft heading toward an unknown, remote island. A deep-purple hue filled the sky along with stratus clouds. Stillness was omnipresent. The only sound emitted was from waves hitting against the raft. The mixture of the seawater and darkness expelled an indescribable scent.

53.

Dawn began casting an over-shadow on the horizon. The result lessened visibility upon the water tremendously. The temperature also began plunging drastically.

Never having experienced the outside world with its mass confusion, Marcus couldn't decide heads or tails of his location. He had no idea as to where he was drifting. The deep waters were quiet and tranquil. His surroundings were unknown. Since his sail, he'd never encountered a living soul. No other boats or aircrafts were sighted. He kept looking behind anticipating the Coast Guards to be in pursuit. Up ahead in the far distance an island came into view. Marcus navigated the small vessel toward the location. He was now exhausted and hungry. *'Maybe I can find help there.'*

***

"This just doesn't make any sense. They can't be that far," stated the director. They were in the command center. The area was fully occupied with technicians. The stations were manned by staff using all their expert knowledge and technology to locate and contain the doctor and X-12. The director was up for hours operating purely on caffeine. His career was riding on the results of the pursuit. He had began to pace. A man wearing a dark suit approached the director as he was in mid sentence with a staff member. The director was handed a document. The dark suited man continued onward. The director read the report. A smile was revealed. There was a break in the search. He was excited again. The Coast Guards reported having contact with the two at sea. The report talked about finding an abandoned ship. The director thought about what X-12 evolved into. After reading the message, his excitement shaped his emotions. *'The first solid confirmation.'* He kept reading. "Okay people! We have a new location to start from. I want aerial support in this area."

A Bell & Howell 500XT helicopter hovered over the sea. It was the scene where the abandoned Coast Guard ship was found. The salty, sea wind was mixed with a misty, spew of water. The force behind the wind gust was from the rotor blades turning at high revolutions. The sound of the motor drowned their conversations onboard. They used headsets to communicate through the din. Other government vessels were visible below in the area.

"This is the quadrant." The director looked around. "Where's the closest inland?"

The pilot began checking his digital map on the dashboard. "Saddle

Wood Bluff. It's a small remote island. I don't think it's inhabited but we shall see." The pilot used his radio to dispatch some of the sea vessels to the area in question.

***

Saddle Wood Bluff is an uncharted island 250 miles off the Eastern Shore. Recently, it was explored and used by marine biologists doing research on undocumented life forms. In recent finds, seven unnamed species were discovered. Marcus continued heading toward the island, As he neared, he could hear faint sounds. The closer he approached, the clearer the sounds became. Suddenly, they became distinctive to his cognizance. The voices were unfamiliar. Embedded in Marcus's subconscious was the process of decoding the expressions.

Marcus moored the boat to a large rock. Walking inland his shoes were saturated by the salty water. Sand greeted his feet as he walked on dry land. Beige sand glistened like crystals off of the moonlight. The sand-filled ground stretched inland for about 100 feet. Afterward, green grass was visible for miles. Marcus's eyes adjusted to the darkness that permeated the island. The voices were silent. He noticed the island had its own presence and sounds. Hundreds of eyes were aglow everywhere. They were from the many different species of the wilderness. Some were documented, some were unknown to man. They felt the presence of the intruder. It was an intrusion far beyond their feeble understanding of coexistence.

As Marcus moved inland, he was surrounded by thousands of eyes from the wildlife. Some, who at other times, would have been at odds with one another for survival. At that moment they were peaceful. Their differences were not important. Although darkness blanketed the island, Marcus was equipped with nocturnal vision as the others. From Marcus' vision, the creatures were displayed in a lime-green hue. They parted a pathway as Marcus walked. The gap was closed afterward. They trailed behind him. It was evident they were paying homage to their Messiah.

54.

The force of the Bell & Howell 500XT rotor blades created a whirlwind of sand and sea mist as it hovered over the beachfront. A pair of amphibian water crafts were heading toward the shore. Inside the vessels were an elite group of special opts rangers. They were dispatched within a moments notice to the area by the director.

The aircraft sat down on the soft grass. The director and an armed, uniformed man exited leaving the pilot with the helicopter. They stood crouched in efforts to avoid contact with the rotating blades above.

"We'll set up perimeters around this place. We'll forge inward. If your boy is here we'll find him." The commander's voice was exaggerated because of the sound of the engine reverberation.

Just then, the water crafts came onto the beachfront. The vessels were equipped with huge wheels. There were eight to be exact. A hatch on both crafts opened simultaneously. Ten armed soldiers stood in formation on the beachfront awaiting orders.

***

Using night vision goggles, the soldiers traveled inland toward the unknown. Strange sounds permeated the area. The sounds of underbrush snapping under their weight intensified in the forest. Scout soldiers took the lead as they crossed a shallow pond. As soon as their feet were submerged in the mirky water, movement was spotted in the water. Bubbles began to form in the pond. Suddenly, the sounds of yells and screams from fear and excruciating pain enveloped the area. The soldiers were unprepared for the intrusion. A sudden onslaught of piranhas were attacking their feet and legs. Sharp teeth with powerful jaws easily penetrated their clothing and flesh. Sharp blast from the soldier's weapons aiming at the water exploded with fire and smoke. Vertical waves developed from the velocity of the projectiles. Some hit their mark, most missed. The men hurried to the other side.

"Damn piranhas! I didn't know they existed in these parts!" exclaimed the commander. He went to attend to the wounded men needing medical support. After first aid was administered, they continued onward.

One hundred yards into the trek, they were attacked again. This time by wasp-like insects. There were thousands of them flying frantically and stopping the men in their path. The soldiers adorned mask and continued forward.

***

Marcus took shelter in a thatched roof hut. He was awakened abruptly because of a disturbing vibration. At first he thought it was part of a dream. He awoke with foreign voices in his head. Suddenly, he understood what was happening. He realized men would be there soon. He sat on the matted ground to meditated.

The soldiers continued forward. The horizon was beginning to show signs of light. Daylight would soon arrive.

"Look!" The sound came over everyone's two-way radio. They stopped in their tracks. Their attention was focused on the view point. Using binoculars equipped with Night Owl lenses, the director saw a hut in the far distance.

Stealthily, the men approached the hut. Silence overshadowed the night. The men took position around the flimsy hut. Their weapons were aimed. They knew the element of surprise was on their side. When the signal was finally given, they stormed the hut. The enclosure was empty. Only a few scurrying lizards were seen trying to escape the invasion.

The commander entered the quarters after it was secured. He picked up the clothing laying on a mat. He held them up. "He was here. He won't get too far. We'll catch him. Gear up and let's get a move on!" he ordered.

The sounds of boots trotting into the woodland was pronounced. A group of lizards watched the soldiers head deeper into the forest from a rock they were perched on.

Marcus knew he must never be captured. The area was now quiet. The sound of the soldier's movements no longer resonated. Suddenly, Marcus began to transform into his human counterpart. The morph took only minutes. He stood naked amongst the other wildlife looking over at them. He knew he was their leader. They were everywhere, in the sea, on the land, and in the air. They all began communicating telepathically.

The species were informed of the evolvement. The heavens parted. A bright, orange-red light beamed from the celestials. The sight was extraordinary and majestical. Darkness surrounded the forest. It was a certain location where the illumination took place. The foreign voices returned to Marcus. The same voices he heard in the boat when he approached inland. This time there was clairvoyance. He knew they were from his ancestors. They were calling him to come home. He was being informed the mission was accomplished. They would survive with mankind without ever being exposed again.

Marcus felt comfort. He headed directly into the beam of light. There was no pain, no sensation, only oneness with his legacy.

Made in the USA
Columbia, SC
19 April 2021